Hippity Hoppity Homicide by

Kathi Daley

D1739241

I want to thank the very talented Jessica Fischer for the cover art.

I so appreciate Bruce Curran, who is always ready and willing to answer my cyber questions; Jayme Maness for helping out with the book clubs; and Peggy Hyndman for helping sleuth out those pesky typos.

And, of course, thanks to the readers and bloggers in my life, who make doing what I do possible.

Thank you to Randy Ladenheim-Gil for the editing.

And a special thanks to Nancy Farris, Jean Daniel, Patty Liu, and Vivian Shane for submitting recipes.

And finally, I want to thank my husband Ken for allowing me time to write by taking care of everything else.

Books by Kathi Daley

Come for the murder, stay for the romance

Zoe Donovan Cozy Mystery:

Halloween Hijinks
The Trouble With Turkeys
Christmas Crazy
Cupid's Curse
Big Bunny Bump-off
Beach Blanket Barbie
Maui Madness
Derby Divas
Haunted Hamlet
Turkeys, Tuxes, and Tabbies
Christmas Cozy
Alaskan Alliance
Matrimony Meltdown
Soul Surrender
Heavenly Honeymoon
Hopscotch Homicide
Ghostly Graveyard
Santa Sleuth
Shamrock Shenanigans
Kitten Kaboodle
Costume Catastrophe
Candy Cane Caper
Holiday Hangover
Easter Escapade
Camp Carter
Trick or Treason
Reindeer Roundup
Hippity Hoppity Homicide

Tj Jensen Paradise Lake Mysteries by Henery Press:

Pumpkins in Paradise
Snowmen in Paradise
Bikinis in Paradise
Christmas in Paradise
Puppies in Paradise
Halloween in Paradise
Treasure in Paradise
Fireworks in Paradise
Beaches in Paradise – *July 2018*

Whales and Tails Cozy Mystery:

Romeow and Juliet
The Mad Catter
Grimm's Furry Tail
Much Ado About Felines
Legend of Tabby Hollow
Cat of Christmas Past
A Tale of Two Tabbies
The Great Catsby
Count Catula
The Cat of Christmas Present
A Winter's Tail
The Taming of the Tabby
Frankencat
The Cat of Christmas Future
Farewell to Felines
The Cat of New Orleans – *June 2018*

Writers' Retreat Southern Seashore Mystery:

First Case
Second Look
Third Strike
Fourth Victim
Fifth Night
Sixth Cabin – *May 2018*

Rescue Alaska Paranormal Mystery:

Finding Justice
Finding Answers – *May 2018*

A Tess and Tilly Mystery:

The Christmas Letter
The Valentine Mystery
The Mother's Day Mishap – *April 2018*

Sand and Sea Hawaiian Mystery:

Murder at Dolphin Bay
Murder at Sunrise Beach
Murder at the Witching Hour
Murder at Christmas
Murder at Turtle Cove
Murder at Water's Edge
Murder at Midnight

Seacliff High Mystery:

The Secret
The Curse
The Relic
The Conspiracy
The Grudge
The Shadow
The Haunting

Haunting by the Sea:

Homecoming by the Sea – *April 2018*

Road to Christmas Romance:

Road to Christmas Past

Chapter 1

Sunday, March 25

The first thing I noticed upon entering the room was that the bedspread didn't match the carpet, which was a totally different color from the drapes. Mismatched decor is an odd thing to have float past your consciousness when you've just been told that a man whose friendship you value is dead and your husband is missing. On an intellectual level I knew I was in shock and the emotions that any rational person should and would experience were waiting just below the surface, but in that moment I felt nothing.

"Zoe, are you okay?" Sheriff Salinger asked.

I looked away from the drapes and stared at him with what I was sure was a confused expression. I knew something was expected of me, but I had no idea what it was everyone was waiting for.

"This is too much for her," my friend, Levi Denton, said. He put his hands on my shoulders, turned my body toward him, and stared into my eyes, a look of concern evident on his face. "She shouldn't be here. There must be another way."

"I don't disagree that it would be best if Zoe didn't need to be here," Salinger said, "but the instructions left by the person or persons who have Zak were very specific."

I averted my eyes from Levi's concerned gaze and looked around the room. There was blood splatter everywhere. My mind began to feel fuzzy as the room seemed to fade in and out. I felt a wave of nausea as I struggled to accept what I'd witnessed with my own eyes. This couldn't be real. It didn't make sense. I put my hand to my face to try to wake myself from this horrible nightmare.

"Zoe?" Levi put a hand on my cheek and gently turned my head so I was looking at him again. He looked so scared. So vulnerable. In that moment I knew this was real and not a dream, as I had hoped. I glanced to the floor and then back to Levi. "How did he die?" I asked as I tried very hard to look away from the outline of Will's body, which had been covered with a sheet.

"Shot in the head," Salinger answered.

I cringed.

"He would have gone quickly, so at least he didn't suffer," Salinger added.

"When?" I asked in a voice so soft I wondered if anyone had heard.

"The 911 call reporting the sound of a gunshot came through about thirty minutes ago," Salinger answered.

I closed my eyes as a single tear slid down my cheek. Thirty minutes ago, I'd been at home feeding my three-month-old daughter, Catherine Donovan Zimmerman, while Scooter Sherwood and Alex Bremmerton, the two children who lived with Zak and me, chatted about the funny thing they'd seen in town that afternoon. Thirty minutes ago, I was making plans for the Easter celebration I planned to host next weekend. Thirty minutes ago I hadn't known that Will was dead or that Zak had been kidnapped by the monster who had killed him.

Levi put his arms around me and pulled me tightly into his chest. I closed my eyes and took comfort in the sound of his strong, steady heartbeat. I knew that giving in to the despair that threatened to overwhelm me wasn't an option. I'd lost a friend today and my heart wanted to weep at the injustice of it. But if the note Salinger held was authentic, Zak was still alive, and it was up to me to save him. I glanced at the sheet on the floor and knew I must set the rage in my soul aside.

"I can take you home if you need some time to process what's happened," Levi offered as I felt my tears soak into his sweater.

I dug down deep for the strength I needed, squeezed him tightly around the waist, and then took a step back. "I'm fine." I turned and looked at Salinger. "What do I need to do?"

I knew he'd found our friend and employee, Will Danner, lying in a pool of blood after receiving an anonymous 911 call. Will, a teacher at Zimmerman Academy, the private school Zak and I owned, had been staying in a motel near the Academy while his house was being remodeled. Zak had agreed to meet him that evening regarding a project on which they were collaborating. When Salinger arrived, he'd found a note in Will's left hand and a burner cell in his right. The note detailed a very specific set of instructions stating that Zoe Donovan Zimmerman, and only Zoe Donovan Zimmerman, was to call the number provided on the piece of paper with the phone that had been left in Will's hand.

"We need to call the number and find out what they want," Salinger said. "There isn't anything we can do to help Will. What we need to focus on is finding Zak."

I swallowed what felt like a boulder in my throat, "I agree." I held out my hand for the phone. Salinger handed it to me and I looked at it and frowned. "There's blood on it. That doesn't seem right."

"Yeah, there's blood everywhere," Levi said.

"No, Zoe's right," Salinger said, looking at both the phone and the note. Salinger pulled back the sheet, causing me to look away as he did. "There's blood splatter on the phone and the note but not on Will's hands beneath the phone and the note."

"And that's important because…?" Levi asked.

"It's important because it suggests Will was already holding them before he was shot," I explained.

Salinger carefully rolled Will's body to one side and I forced myself to watch. "There isn't any blood beneath his torso," Salinger confirmed.

Levi paled. "Are you telling me some wacko made Will lay on his back holding the phone and note and then shot him in the head?"

"It could have occurred that way, but it's more likely Will was already unconscious when he was shot," Salinger explained.

"I guess that's a good thing," Levi mumbled.

I looked at the phone again. I knew once I started there was no going back. I had no idea where this first phone call would lead, but I had a feeling I was in for a bumpy ride. Nothing else made sense. The setup had been much too elaborate for an easy and painless conclusion to be on the horizon.

I looked at Levi again. He frowned, but I could see he was struggling to be strong for me. "I guess we should do this."

He nodded.

I looked at Salinger. "Are you ready?"

Salinger nodded. "Hold the phone away from your ear so we can hear what's being said as well."

I nodded and pushed the Call button on the phone that had already been programmed. After only one ring a deep voice that sounded unreal came on the line. The message seemed to have been prerecorded using an automated voice system.

"Welcome to The Sleuthing Game. The purpose of the game is to solve the eight puzzles you will be provided before the allotted time for each runs out. If you are successful, your husband will be returned to you unharmed. If you are unsuccessful you will never see the father of your child alive again. The first set of instructions, as well as the first puzzle, has been taped to the bottom of one of the tables at the Classic Cue pool hall. You have until eight p.m. this evening to retrieve and follow the instructions. No cops or Zak dies."

I glanced at Salinger. "What sort of sicko are we dealing with?"

Salinger frowned. "I don't know."

"It makes no sense that anyone would shoot one man and then kidnap a second one simply to make Zoe engage in a ridiculous game of some sort," Levi stated.

"Do you really think whoever is behind this will kill Zak if I refuse to play?" I asked, fighting the dizziness that threatened to thrust me into a state of unconsciousness. I took a deep breath and fought the urge to slide into the darkness. Focusing on Salinger as he looked around the room, I felt the dizziness dissipate.

"I don't know," he repeated. "But given the fact that he or she has already killed once, I think we have to assume they will."

"Who would do such a thing?" Levi asked a question that had been asked before and I knew would be asked a dozen times more before this was over.

"It's obviously personal," I said as I felt my strength begin to return. "Someone wants to make me jump through a bunch of hoops. I'm going to assume we're dealing with someone I've harmed in the past. The fact that they're referring to their sick ploy as The Sleuthing Game indicates to me that the person behind this is most likely someone I helped put in jail." I looked at Levi. "I need to do this. I can't risk Zak's life by not cooperating. I need you and Ellie to stay with the kids until this is over."

"You can't do this alone."

"I think I have to. I don't want Ellie and the kids to be alone. I need you to be with them."

I could see Levi wanted to argue, but then Salinger spoke. "I'm going to call the county office to see if I can get a couple of deputies to watch your house."

"Thank you. I'll feel better about things if I know the kids are safe and this psycho can't grab one of them next, if that's what they plan." I glanced at my watch. "I need to get a move on if I'm going to find the next set of instructions before the deadline."

"I'll run home and change into plainclothes," Salinger said. "I'll borrow my neighbor's car as well. I'll follow you from a distance."

"What if they see you?" I asked.

"They won't."

"The voice on the phone specifically said no cops," Levi stated. "I know you said you were going to change out of your uniform, but the person who's doing this probably knows what you look like. I think I should be the one to follow Zoe."

I looked toward Levi and shook my head vigorously. "I don't want to put you in any danger. This madman wants me and only me. I need to do this alone."

I couldn't help but notice the look of resolve that crossed Levi's face. "I'm not letting you do this alone. That isn't an option. Someone has to go with you and because the voice on the phone said no cops that someone can't be Salinger."

"But…"

Levi grabbed my shoulders. He forced me to face him. I could see he was as determined to help me as I was for him to be safely out of harm's way. "I'm going with you. I know you don't think you need me, but you do. I know you think you'll be putting me in danger, but you won't. You said yourself this seems to be some sick game between you and whoever is orchestrating it. I doubt they'll have a bit of interest in me."

My resolve hardened. "If it's personal between me and this person why did they kill Will?"

"To get your attention," Levi answered. "To demonstrate the lengths to which they'll go if you don't comply with their instructions. Please." Levi looked me directly in the eye. "I'm going with you. Don't fight me on this."

I glanced at Salinger. "What do you think?"

Salinger shrugged. "I suppose Levi has a good point. You most likely will need help, and as much as I'd like to provide it, maybe he should be the one to go with you. The last thing we want to do is make whoever is behind this angry by ignoring the no-cops dictate. I'll head over to your house and stay with Ellie and the kids until the guys from the county show up. Levi can call me after you retrieve the next set of instructions. I think right now we need to do what the kidnappers are asking to the best of our ability. Once we know what they're really after we can work together to come up with a plan."

"Okay." I looked at Levi, having come to a decision. "Let's go."

The drive between the motel where the attack had occurred and the Classic Cue was accomplished in silence. It took every ounce of strength I could muster not to curl into a fetal position and sob until the sweet peace of unconsciousness overcame me. The thought that Zak was being held by a crazy person filled me with more terror than my mind was able to process and I knew it was only a matter of time before my determination slipped and a feeling of helplessness returned.

I closed my eyes and took a deep breath. I needed to calm my mind so I could focus. I needed to stay strong for Zak. I let my mind wander until eventually it landed on a thought about Catherine and the prebedtime feeding the two of us enjoyed each evening. Catherine knew Ellie and I supposed she would be fine with favorite honorary auntie putting her to bed, but in the three months since she was born I'd never missed a single bedtime feeding.

Given what was going on, it was a good thing I'd been forced to stop breast feeding. I'd felt like a total failure when I learned my body wasn't producing enough of the nutrients my baby needed, but now that I wouldn't be able to be with Catherine for however long this sick, sick game took to complete, I was glad she was used to taking a bottle. It would have been a lot harder on both of us if we hadn't already made the transition.

"We're almost there," Levi said, breaking into my daydream.

I sat up and opened my eyes. "When we get to the Classic Cue I'll go in and find the next set of instructions while you call Ellie. I know Salinger said he was going to head over to the house, but she must be frantic."

"Yeah, I'm sure she probably is."

"Tell her that Alex knows where everything she'll need to take care of Catherine is. And tell her to keep the kids home from school tomorrow. I don't want them to go out at all until we're able to track this guy down and put him safely behind bars."

"Okay. I'll tell her." Levi turned onto the street where the pool hall was located. "Maybe we can figure out who he is and where he's holding Zak. If we can find him we can end this. At some point he's bound to make a mistake, give something away."

I glanced out the passenger side window. Familiar buildings passed as we slowly made our way down the street. It was cool this evening, so the sidewalks were sparsely populated; still, it seemed odd that there were people going about their normal lives completely unaware of the fact that Will was dead and Zak was missing. "Yeah," I whispered as Levi stopped at a crosswalk. "We should keep our ears open. The sooner this is over the better."

We arrived at the pool hall and I went in alone. Levi and I weren't certain how the killer would react to his presence, so we decided it was best for him to hang in the background. The pool hall was crowded and the tables were all occupied, which was going to make searching for a note taped beneath one of them difficult. I walked up to the first table, where two men who looked to be in their early twenties were engaged in a game of eight ball. "I'm sorry to interrupt your game, but I need to crawl under your table for just a minute."

"Did you lose something, sweetheart?" one of the men asked after looking me up and down with a suggestive grin on his face.

"I dropped an earring the last time I was here," I lied. "I'll only be a minute."

The men stepped back and I got down on my hands and knees. I tried to ignore the catcalls as I slipped under the table. Yes, I realized my jeans-covered backside was sticking up in the air in a most unfortunate position, but I had little choice in positioning my body as I tried to move around in the tight space. Unfortunately, I didn't find the note, so I thanked the men, then went to the next table and repeated the humiliating process. There were sixteen tables in the room, which would mean a lot of time crawling around on the dirty floor with my butt in the air if the note happened to be taped to the last one I checked. Luckily, I found both a note and a cell phone taped to the undercarriage of the eighth table I crawled beneath. I grabbed both and headed out to the car.

The note contained a set of instructions along with a riddle that, when solved, would lead me to a location. The note indicated that the phone would ring at exactly 9:14. I was to answer it on the third ring. If I had solved the puzzle and ended up in the correct place I would have the information I needed to be able to answer the second question. Once I provided the answer I would be given nine additional minutes to provide five additional answers.

"Okay, so what's the riddle?" Levi asked.

"'To find the clue you must peel back the letters and find that which remains,'" I read aloud.

"Huh?" Levi asked. "What on earth does that mean?"

"I think it's suggesting there's a hidden message contained within the riddle. Or maybe invisible ink was used to write something on the back." I continued to stare at the piece of paper in my hand. The psycho who had gone to all the trouble of orchestrating the game wanted me to play, so they wouldn't have started off with a riddle I couldn't solve.

"Peel back the words," Levi said as he held out his hand, indicating I should give him the note. "Maybe he wants us to focus on part of what's provided. I notice there seem to be a lot of pretty specific numbers."

I thought about the note. The fact that he wanted me to pick up on the third ring and answer the second question was unusual, as was the time of nine-fourteen for the phone call.

"Okay; what numbers are mentioned in order?" I asked. I took out my phone to record them.

"The instructions state that you'll get a call at 9:14, so that's 9-1-4. Then you pick up on the third ring and answer the second question, so that gives us 9-1-4-3-2. After that you'll be given nine minutes to answer five more questions."

"That's 9-1-4-3-2-9-5," I said aloud. 'I know where we need to go."

"Where?" Levi asked.

"It's Zak's private line at Zimmerman Academy."

Chapter 2

"Do you have your key?" Levi asked as he pulled away from the curb and headed back down the street. "Chances are the person behind the game wants you in Zak's office, not just in the parking lot of the school."

"No, I don't." I looked at my watch. "When you showed up at my house I just ran out the door and didn't even bother to grab my purse. Phyllis lives close to the Academy. I'll call her to see if she can meet us there and let us in."

Luckily, Phyllis King, the principal and administrator at the Academy, was at home and was able to meet us and let us in the door. I'd told her time was of the essence, so she hadn't asked a lot of questions, though I had a feeling I'd need to come up with some answers by the time we arrived at the school. Phyllis and Will had been romantically involved at one point, and while they no longer dated, they'd remained friends. She'd take the news of his death hard.

I called Salinger while Levi merged onto the highway and headed toward Zimmerman Academy. He wasn't at all thrilled with sitting on the sidelines, but I did my best to assure him that so far Levi and I had this game nailed down and the thing I most needed him to do was to make sure my family was safe.

I still wasn't sure how the person behind the game was going to feel about the fact that I was getting help from my friends, but I had in my possession two cell phones provided by them, and if they had a problem with Levi helping me, they could call and tell me so.

Phyllis was waiting in her car near the front of the school when Levi and I pulled up.

"Thank you so much," I said, then grabbed the key and ran toward the door. I had exactly one minute to make it to Zak's office. I was sure Phyllis was confused as she watched me go, but I didn't have time to explain if I was going to make my deadline. At exactly nine-fourteen the burner cell I'd found taped to the table at the pool hall rang. I waited until the third ring and answered. I was again met with a deep automated voice.

"Are you in the office?"

"I am," I said, although I wasn't sure if anyone was listening on the other end or the whole thing was automated. That must be question number one because the note said I'd need to locate information to answer number two.

"Turn on the phone's GPS," the voice instructed.

I went into the settings and did as I was told.

"Good," the voice said. *"Now, I want you to go to the file cabinet and look for a file labeled CASS. After you retrieve it I want you to turn to the first page and find the project number. It should begin with NS and be followed by nine numbers. When you get that text it to the only contact the cell you picked up has programmed into it. You have two minutes. When the code is received the phone will ring again with the next set of instructions."*

I set the phone on the desk and hurried over to the row of file cabinets. There was a wall of plexiglass in front of it. The wall, which was really more of a door, was locked. I knew Zak hid a key in the monkey paperweight Alex had given him on her first Christmas with us. I unlocked the glass door, then opened the first drawer in the first file cabinet and hurriedly searched for the file. Unfortunately, Zak had a lot of files.

"What are we looking for?" Levi asked as he slipped into the office, with Phyllis trailing behind him. He must have filled her in on the situation because it was obvious she'd been crying.

"I need to find a file labeled CASS. Zak has a lot of files and I only have two minutes—actually, less than two minutes now—to find the file and the project number, and text it to the psycho pulling the strings."

Phyllis and Levi each opened a file cabinet and began looking. Hopefully, one of us would find it in time. After about a minute Phyllis announced she had found the file. I opened it and looked for the project number. The voice had said it would begin with NS.

"Do you know what CASS stands for?" Levi asked as he looked at the file over my shoulder.

"No idea. The voice on the phone didn't ask me that, so I think finding the project number is the most important thing." I quickly scanned the page and found the number the caller had asked for.

"CASS stands for Classified Arial Surveillance System," Levi said as I began to type in the numbers following NS. "And I think NS stands for National Security or some such thing."

I paused after typing in the last number. All I needed was to hit Send. "I don't care," I said as I hit it. "It's Zak's life we're talking about."

"Yeah, I get it," Levi said, although he looked somewhat less certain than I felt that we'd done the right thing by giving the psycho the information he wanted.

After a few seconds the phone rang. I answered. Again, I was greeted by a deep computer-generated voice. This time it told me to look through the files for one labeled MGGS. I was to once again find the NS number and text it. This time he only gave me one minute. At least now I knew what I was looking for and where to find it. After I provided the project number for Military Grade Guidance System I was asked to find four additional files for other projects Zak had worked on at some point in his career. I had to admit I had no idea he was involved in so much secret military stuff. A quick glance at the dates on the files indicated they were associated with old projects he'd worked on before we'd even been married. Still, in all the years we'd been together he'd never said anything that would lead me to believe he had a high security clearance.

After I delivered all the file numbers I received a final call instructing me to destroy the burner cell, head to Lucky's Bar, and wait for the final set of instructions for the evening.

"Final set?" I said aloud. "The initial instructions indicated I would have eight tasks to do. Surely they aren't going to drag this out over several days!"

"It kind of sounds like that's exactly what they're intending," Levi said. "We should go."

"I'm coming with you," Phyllis said. "I have a lot of questions. You can answer them on the way."

I wasn't sure whether whoever was behind this game cared that Levi was helping me, and I certainly wasn't sure they'd be okay with two helpers, but Phyllis had helped us out in a crunch and she deserved some answers to her questions. As soon as Levi took off toward town, I began filling Phyllis in on what we knew. I was sure she was horrified to find out what had happened to Will, but I reminded her that there wasn't anything we could do to help him, though we could help Zak, which had to be our top priority.

"Who do you think is doing this?" Phyllis asked as tears streamed down her face. My heart bled for her. Phyllis had chosen career over marriage at an early age and as far as I knew, Will had been the first man she'd given her heart to despite the fact that she was well into her sixties before love had finally found her.

"I don't know," I answered. "Initially, The Sleuthing Game theme led me to believe someone I may have helped Salinger arrest could be behind it. The fact that whoever's pulling the strings wanted files related to national security makes me wonder if I was wrong. I'm beginning to think whoever has Zak is a big-time criminal, not some small-town killer."

"You said Zak was kidnapped from the motel where Will's been staying. Do you know why they were meeting?" Phyllis asked.

I glanced at her. I could see she was fighting to stay focused on the specifics of what was going on. Like me, I imagined she felt it was easier to engage the analytical side of her brain for now. "I don't know all the details, but it seems Zak and Will must have been working on some sort of a secret project together. Zak never shared the details, but I'm pretty sure Zak was approached with the project and he brought Will in to help him with the mathematical calculations. That's really all I know."

"But why did they meet today?" Phyllis continued. "It's Sunday and a day off for both men. They would have been at work at the Academy tomorrow. What was so important that it couldn't have waited a few hours?"

My brows furrowed. "Good question. I don't know why Zak went over to Will's motel room today." I turned and looked directly at Phyllis, who was sitting in the backseat. "Do you think the fact that they were working on a Sunday is important?"

Phyllis was a tall woman with strong features, but in that moment she looked small and fragile. She shrugged. "It seems important to me, although I don't have all the pieces. I do wonder how whoever is doing this knew they were at the motel."

"Maybe the killer arranged for the meeting to occur in the first place," Levi suggested.

"I guess that's possible," I answered. "Alex and Scooter wanted to go into town today, and I'd been fighting a headache all day, so I decided to lay down while Catherine was napping. When I got up I found a note from Zak saying he went to meet Will but would be home for dinner. The next thing I knew, Levi was at my door, telling me that Salinger had called and asked him to bring me to the motel. Salinger said there'd been an incident, although I didn't know how bad things were until I arrived. Still, I knew Salinger wouldn't call me without an important reason, so I asked Alex to keep an eye on Catherine and left right away, which is why I didn't have my purse or my key to the Academy."

"And this man told you that he would kill Zak if you didn't do exactly what he said?" Phyllis asked.

"That's what he said. At this point that's what I have to believe."

Phyllis wiped a tear from her cheek, but another quickly replaced it. "I wonder why he didn't take Will as well?" Phyllis's voice caught in her throat. "Why did he have to kill him?"

"I wish I had the answers you need, but all I have now are questions."

"I wonder if he suffered," Phyllis said in a soft voice.

"Salinger said he hadn't," I answered.

"I pray he's at peace."

I smiled gently at Phyllis and then called Salinger to give him an update on the situation. He was still at my house, but he assured me that plainclothes deputies were on the way to keep an eye on it and the people within.

When we arrived at the bar I insisted on going in alone. I still wasn't sure if the man with the deep voice knew I had friends helping me or would care if he did. I figured it was best not to announce it if I didn't need to. After entering the bar I paused and looked around. The place was packed. The only instruction was to go to the bar. I had no idea what I was supposed to do once I got there.

An old woman who'd been sitting at the bar got up and approached me. She handed me a large envelope and told me that a man had come in and asked her to hold it until a woman came in looking for it. I asked her how she knew I was that woman and she said the man had shown her a photo of me holding a baby.

My heart sank. Apparently, this madman knew about Catherine. The urge to grab her and flee the country was strong, but I needed to help Zak. I tried to get a description of the man, but all the woman could remember was that he was tall with dark hair. I thanked her and headed out to the car.

"So, what do we have now?" Levi asked after I slid into the passenger seat.

I opened the envelope. Inside was a note, a thumb drive, and another burner phone. The note instructed me to access the drive and decrypt the message. I had until six a.m. the next morning to be ready with the answer. "Six a.m.?" I screeched. "What about Zak? Am I supposed to just wait around for this guy to play his silly game?"

"I'm not sure what else we can do," Levi said.

God, I was never going to be able to hold it together if this game went on and on. I needed to end it. I needed to have Zak with me now!

"I'm not going to be any help at decrypting a code delivered via a thumb drive, but I do want to help," Phyllis offered. "Please let me know what I can do."

"I don't think there's anything right now, but I do appreciate the offer," I answered.

Phyllis glanced down at her hands and then up at me. "I suppose I'll plan to be at the Academy tomorrow morning. It seems important that someone be there to explain about Mr. Danner. It should be me. But please don't hesitate to call if there's anything at all I can do. I want to help. I need to help. I'm sure once I speak to the staff, Ethan and the others will want to help as well."

"Thanks," I said. "I'll call you tomorrow no matter what. I'm going to have Levi drop me at home and then he can run you back to your car."

By the time I got home I was exhausted, but there was no way I was going to be able to sleep a wink until Zak was back with me. Catherine, and Levi and Ellie's son, Eli, had long since been put down for the night. Scooter was asleep on the sofa in front of the TV, but Ellie and Alex were both up and waiting for us to return. I could see they had been crying and I wanted to be able to assure them that things would be okay, but I wasn't sure about anything.

"Levi ran Phyllis back to her car, which she left at the Academy, but he'll be here after that," I informed them. "I'm going to look in on Catherine, and after that I have a thumb drive to download and decode."

"Oh good. Something I can do to help." Alex held out her hand. I hesitated just a minute, then handed her the drive. She could run circles around me when it came to anything technology-related and I really wanted to get this game over with as quickly as possible.

Alex went into the computer room and I headed upstairs. I fought back the tears I absolutely refused to give in to. I knew if I started crying I would never be able to stop. When I arrived at the door to the nursery

I found my dog Charlie sleeping in front of it. I should have known he would be there. If I was home Charlie was most often with me, but when I was away he spent most of his time keeping an eye on Catherine,

I bent down and greeted my best buddy. I buried my face in his soft fur and took comfort in his presence. "I should have known you'd be up here protecting our girl."

Charlie licked my face. Before Catherine was born I'd worried he would be jealous of the small human who would occupy so much of my time, but from the moment I brought her home from the hospital it was obvious he loved and felt protective of her.

I kissed Charlie on the top of his head, stood up, and opened the nursery door. He followed me inside. Catherine was wrapped in a blanket and sleeping on her stomach. I gently placed a hand on her head of dark hair and watched her even breathing. God, I loved her. Before I gave birth I hadn't understood the depth of emotion I would feel when I held her in my arms. Catherine had changed something in me. Something primal. I'm not sure I can explain what that something was exactly, but my mothering instincts had been awakened, and I knew I wanted to be a better person. I had this small, helpless person who depended on me for everything, and from the moment she was placed in my arms, I knew the most important thing in my life was my commitment to her, my promise to her to become the mother she needed and deserved.

Of course, the most important thing I needed to do now was to make sure her daddy came home to her. I leaned forward and kissed her on the head, being careful not to wake her. I paused to make sure the baby monitor was on and the window to her room was closed and locked, and then went back downstairs with Charlie on my heels to find out how Alex was doing with the thumb drive.

"The drive is password protected, but I can get in with a little time," Alex said. She had a serious look on her face as she bit her lip while entering commands into the computer at a rate I was certain even Zak would have a hard time keeping up with. "I'm pretty sure once I get in I'll find the document is encoded, because whoever's behind this seems to want to challenge you, but I don't want you to worry. I *will* decode the document and get you the information you need to save Zak."

Alex spoke with such confidence and conviction, I couldn't help but feel proud. She'd always been a genius, but under Zak's tutelage she'd blossomed into a confident young woman who had mad computer skills and would probably one day rule the world. Or at least the cyberworld. Socially, she was still very much a thirteen-year-old girl with blossoming emotions and corresponding insecurities.

"If the point of this little game is to cause you to jump through hoops why would they give you a task to complete that you aren't capable of?" Ellie asked.

"Good question." I looked at Alex. If she hadn't been home and willing to help me there was no way I would have been able to access the drive or decode the document. Had the person behind the game known she was here and that I'd seek her help? The thought gave me little comfort. The last thing I'd wanted to do was bring Alex into this mess, but it was beginning to look as if her presence had been taken in to consideration all along.

"We've been asking ourselves if the person behind this cares if you get help. Perhaps this is your answer," Levi pointed out. "The message said no cops, but at no time were you instructed to come alone."

I narrowed my gaze. "That's a good point. Maybe the person expected me to use all the resources available to me, including my friends." I glanced at Ellie. "Has Salinger left?"

"Yes, about fifteen minutes before you arrived. There are two plainclothes officers outside keeping an eye on things."

"Okay, good. I have a feeling whoever is behind this can see what we're doing. Maybe they have hidden cameras or something. I want to be sure we don't do anything that would get Zak killed."

"I'm in," Alex said. She stopped typing and took a minute to look at the screen. "I've found the password. And just as I thought, the information on the drive is encrypted."

"Can you break it?" I asked, scared to death she wouldn't be up to the task.

"I'll need a little time, but I'll get you the information you need." Alex bit her lip as she stared at the screen. "This looks familiar. I think Zak has a program on his computer to deal with this type of encryption." Alex saved the document and then sent it to Zak's computer. She moved across the room and logged on at his station. As soon as she was settled, she went back to work.

"Is there anything I can do?" Ellie asked me after Alex had turned her attention back to the task before her. "Can I get you something to eat?"

I shook my head. "I'm not hungry."

"I feel so helpless. I wish there was more I could do."

I took Ellie's hand in mine. "It's important to me that I know Catherine is safe and cared for. She knows you. It helps a lot that I don't have to worry about her."

Ellie hugged me. "I'll take good care of her. I promise."

"I know you will." I glanced at Levi. "Scooter is sleeping on the sofa in the family room. Maybe you can carry him upstairs to his bed."

"Yeah, okay." Levi glanced at Ellie and gave her a tired smile.

"I'll make some coffee," Ellie offered. "I have a feeling this is going to be a long night."

After Levi and Ellie left the room I sat down on the sofa. I felt tears at the back of my eyes as I watched Alex work. It was better when I was busy. When I had even a moment to think about things I started to panic. I knew that giving in to the hysteria I was fighting very hard to contain wouldn't help anyone, but the thought of Zak at the hands of a madman was about to drive me to the brink of insanity. Maybe that was the point. It did seem that whoever had Zak was intent on punishing me. I just hoped this need to hurt me wouldn't result in the death of the man I loved.

"I think I have it," Alex called out. "I'm in. I've decrypted the document."

I got up and walked across the room. I stood behind Alex and looked over her shoulder at the screen. "What is it?"

"Mathematical equations."

"It doesn't look like any kind of math I've ever seen."

Alex bit her lip. "It's pretty advanced stuff. I might be able to do it, but it would go faster if I had help."

Normally in this situation I would suggest either Zak or Will, but with both unavailable we needed another option. "Who do you want?" I asked.

"Brady is good with the applied stuff, but this is strictly theoretical," Alex said, referring to one of the math teachers at the Academy, Brady Matthews. "I think we'd be better off with Diego." Diego Bradford was a new student. Like Alex, he was younger than most of the other students at fourteen and, like Alex, he was a total genius. I was sure he would do well at any college in the country, but his parents, like Zak and me, didn't want him going there before he could even drive. We both agreed that social and emotional development with age-appropriate peers was equally as important as a stellar education, which was why we'd founded the Academy in the first place.

I didn't know Diego well, but Zak had mentioned that before starting at the Academy this past January, he'd been asked to participate in a project of some sort for NASA. If I had to guess it wouldn't be long before even the teachers here wouldn't be able to keep up with him. Still, for the time being, the Academy was a good option for the gifted young man.

"Are you sure?" I asked. "I thought the two of you didn't get along."

"We don't. He's cocky and arrogant and everything he says rubs me the wrong way, but he's a brilliant mathematician."

"Okay. I'll call Phyllis and have her get hold of him."

"No need." Alex took out her phone and sent off a quick text.

"I wasn't aware you and Diego were texting buddies."

Alex shrugged. "The guy's a jerk, but that doesn't mean I'm beneath asking for his opinion from time to time. I'm better with the computer stuff than he is, but no one in the entire school except for Zak and Will can work an equation the way he does."

Alex's phone dinged. She looked at it. "He's on his way over. I guess you should tell the guys Salinger sent over to let him in."

"How is he getting here?" I asked.

"He was at the arcade when I texted. He said he'd have one of his friends bring him over. He should be here in about fifteen minutes. I'm going to run upstairs for a minute. I'll be back down before he gets here."

I headed outside to let the guys guarding the house know that a fourteen-year-old boy who would most likely arrive in a car driven by another teenager was on his way over and to let him in. After I'd delivered the message I took a few steps toward the beach. There was still snow on the ground, but it hadn't been a season of heavy precipitation, so most of it had melted. I realized the dogs might not have been out for quite some time, so I headed back inside to round up Levi and Ellie's dogs, Shep and Karloff, as well as the three Zimmerman dogs. I could ask Levi to take them out, but I needed a few minutes to pull myself together. I knew tomorrow was going to be a long and difficult day and there wasn't anything I could do until Alex and Diego solved the mathematical equations and we figured out how the answers related to everything else that was going on.

As I strolled along the familiar stretch of sand, I felt the wall of defense I had built against the emotions that threatened to overwhelm me begin to melt away. "Zak," I whispered as tears began to stream down my face. What if I couldn't save him? What if I made a mistake and he died? I couldn't live with that.

I paused and looked out over the dark blue water. There was a slight breeze, which caused ripples on the surface. I remembered the first time Zak and I had come out onto the beach, intending to go skinny-dipping, shortly after I'd moved in with him. The water had been cold, causing goose bumps to break out from head to toe on my body, but he'd been warm. And strong. And welcoming.

I fell to my knees and began to sob. The pent-up emotion I'd been barely controlling overwhelmed me. Zak was my anchor. My home. My life. I felt weak and helpless against the challenge ahead of me, but I had to endure. I had to dig deep and find the strength I feared I didn't have. I couldn't begin to count the number of times Zak had saved me. In fact, Zak saving me had become something of a theme in our relationship. Today, however, it would be up to me to save him.

I let go of the terror I'd been holding at bay and cried out all the fear. All the pain. I screamed at the injustice of it all and prayed for the strength and courage it would take. I wept until I had no more tears to shed. Drained yet resolved, I stood and headed back the way I'd come.

By the time the dogs and I returned to the house, Alex and Diego were sitting in front of the computer side by side. Someone had written a series of numbers and letters on the large whiteboard attached to one wall. It looked like gibberish to me, but based on the smiles on the faces of the teens, they had a good handle on what they were doing and where they were headed.

I went into the den to find Levi sleeping on the sofa. Ellie had gone upstairs when we'd heard Eli crying through the monitor. I decided not to wake Levi because I was sure tomorrow would be a long day for him as well. I picked up Charlie and headed back into the computer room. I pulled a quilt over my legs, tucking Charlie in beside me, then settled in to watch the geniuses work.

It was four a.m. before we had the answers we needed. What I didn't know was whether the solutions to the equations were the answers the voice on the phone wanted, or if they were simply clues that would lead us to something else. I had no idea what that something else might be, so I sent Alex up to bed and made up a guest room for Diego. He lived in the dorm at Zimmerman Academy, but until Zak was home safely I thought it best to keep him close at hand. Plus, I'd noticed he had a way of cutting the tension, at least as far as Alex was concerned. They might not get along socially, but they worked well together, seeming to bring out the best in each other on an academic basis. I remembered when I'd first met Zak in the seventh grade. Like Diego, he was smart and somewhat cocky, and like Alex, I'd hated him on sight. It wasn't until we were both adults that I'd begun to look at him with different eyes. Once I let go of my need to compete with the man who'd been way out of my league from day one, I'd realized the contempt I'd always felt for him was really thinly veiled attraction and admiration.

Chapter 3

Monday, March 26

I was a bundle of nerves by the time six o'clock rolled around. I'd talked it over with Levi, Alex, and Diego, and they'd all agreed it was most likely the person running the game simply wanted the answers to what had turned out to be three very complex equations. That made sense, but because I wasn't completely sure they were correct in their assumption, I wouldn't be able to relax until the answers were provided and accepted.

At exactly six I received a text instructing me to send the answers to the equations to that number. I was too nervous to type and was afraid of making a mistake, so Diego did it for me. For a fourteen-year-old, the kid was cool under pressure. Once the answers had been sent I stood nervously waiting for whatever would happen next. Sixty seconds later the burner phone rang.

"You have done well so far," the computer-generated voice said. *"You will find the next puzzle as well as the next burner phone in the public library. When you arrive seek Neumann's advice. You have until seven fifty-two to find the clue and solve the puzzle."*

"Neumann's advice. What does that mean?" I asked with a touch of hysteria in my voice.

"Chances are he means John von Neumann. He was a mathematician who lived in the first half of the twentieth century," Diego explained. "He was a child prodigy who could do very complicated mental arithmetic at an early age. As an adult, he was an essential pioneer of both quantum physics and computer science. I'm sure there must be a book about him in the library. If you find the book, I think you'll find the next clue."

I swallowed the breath that had lodged in my throat. "Alex, call Hazel and tell her to meet us at the library. Tell her to hurry. She's an early riser, so she should be up already, but if she doesn't answer keep trying until she does." I looked at Levi. "Start the car. I'll be right there."

"Maybe I should go with you," Diego suggested. "If the clue leads to a mathematician, you may have additional equations to solve."

"I don't want to put you or Alex in any danger. Wait here, but stay by the phone. If I need you we'll call." I leaned in toward Diego and lowered my voice. "Take care of Alex. I know she's terrified about what might happen with Zak. Keep her preoccupied."

Diego winked. "You can count on me. I know just how to push her buttons."

"Hazel is on her way," Alex said after disconnecting her phone. "She's curious, of course, about what's going on. I told her you'd explain when you got there."

"Okay, I'm off. I'll call you later, but whatever you do, don't leave the house for any reason. Understand?"

Alex nodded. "You don't have to worry about me, Zoe. I know what's at stake. Diego and I will wait for your call."

When we arrived at the library I asked Hazel about John Von Neumann. She didn't have a biography of him, but she had a book about the greatest mathematicians of all time. She showed us to it, and there was a piece of paper tucked into the page covering John von Neumann's life. Tucked behind the book was another burner cell.

"The person who has Zak must have been here," I realized. "Probably yesterday. They wouldn't want to risk the book being checked out."

"This book hasn't been checked out for years," Hazel informed me. "But I agree. The person who put the note in the book most likely did so recently. But we were closed yesterday."

"Okay, so it must have been on Saturday. You were open until noon then. Do you remember seeing anyone in this section?" I asked.

Hazel thought about it. "Not specifically. It was slow on Saturday. A group of kids came in who needed to find some books for a school report. Other than that, I don't remember seeing anyone in the reference section at all. There were a couple of women browsing the romance section, but that was it."

I doubted whoever we were after was a teenager, but they might have paid one of the kids to put the note in the book. "Do you remember who the kids were?"

Hazel hesitated. "Not offhand, but I can compile a list of everyone who checked books out."

"Okay, great. Call Alex and give her the names. She and Diego can follow up. If a teen was paid to put the note in the book they'd probably be more likely to come clean with them anyway."

Hazel stepped away to make the call.

I looked down at the note and read it out loud. "'Tom and Joe are both kidnapped. Each is isolated, with no means of communicating with the other. Each is offered the opportunity to either gain their freedom by sacrificing the other or to spare the other to achieve the least objectionable outcome. If Tom and Joe both choose to spare the other, they both will be set free. If Tom and Joe both choose to sacrifice the other, they will both die. If Tom chooses to sacrifice Joe, but Joe chooses to spare Tom, Tom will be set free and Joe will die. If Joe chooses to sacrifice Tom, but Tom chooses to spare Joe, Joe will be set free and Tom will die. You are Tom. What would you do?'" I looked at Levi with what I was sure was a blank expression on my face. "Huh?"

"I guess the person behind the game wants you to choose."

"I'm assuming there's only one correct answer?"

Levi shrugged. "You got me. Maybe you should call Alex. This sounds like one of those psychological experiments academics occasionally do."

I took Levi's suggestion and called Alex. She was still on the house phone with Hazel, so she hung up and called me back on her cell. She put me on speaker and I read the message.

"That's classic game theory," Diego said.

"John von Neumann invented game theory," Alex added.

"So what do I do?" I asked. "What's the correct answer?"

"There really isn't a correct answer," Alex explained. "In game theory you have to make a choice based on what you know about the other person and how you think they'll respond."

"Great, because I have no idea who Tom or Joe are."

"The names are placeholders. What if Tom was replaced with Zoe and Joe was replaced with Ellie?" Alex postulated.

I paused and frowned. "Let me be sure I understand this. Assuming Tom and Joe are Ellie and me, if we choose to spare each other we'd both be set free."

"Basically, yes."

"I'd choose to spare Ellie. Ellie would do the same for me and we'd both be set free."

"What if Tom or Joe is Mr. Baker from the market?"

Carl Baker seemed like a nice, honest man. I didn't know him well, but he was pleasant and didn't seem the sort to choose to sacrifice a person to gain his own freedom, although I didn't have a clue what he would do in this situation. "I guess I would still choose to spare him even though I don't know him well to be certain what he would do in that situation.

In fact, I would choose to spare the other person no matter who that was unless I had reason to believe they wouldn't do the same."

"Okay, I'll choose the option to spare Joe and see what happens," Alex said.

At seven fifty-two the burner cell I'd found with the note pinged. I had a text that told me to enter my answer. I texted that I would spare Joe. My text was immediately replied to with the following message: *There is a second captive in addition to Zak. His name is Fred and his wife is Wilma. The game will change a bit. This time Wilma has been given the same puzzle. If you both reply to this text with the word* pain *each man will be given an electrical shock that will hurt quite a lot but not kill them. If Zoe replies with the word* Zak, *and Wilma replies with the word* Fred, *both Zak and Fred will die. If Zoe replies with the word* Zak *and Wilma replies with* pain, *Zak will be set free and Fred will die. If Wilma replies with* Fred *and Zoe replies with* pain, *Fred will go free and Zak will die. You have 60 seconds to reply.*

"Oh God. What do I do?" I asked Levi and Hazel, who were both standing next to me. I knew Alex and Diego were still listening as well via the phone. Panic gripped me as I struggled for the answer. "I don't know Fred or Wilma. I have no idea what Wilma will do."

Everyone was silent. The stakes were too high to just guess, but I only had about thirty more seconds.

"Levi?" I asked as my heart pounded in my chest. I was pretty sure I was going to pass out. How could I guess with Zak's life at stake? What if I guessed wrong?

Levi took my hands in his. He looked me in the eye. "I can't tell you what to do. You'll have to live with the consequences. The choice has to be yours."

"Zak would want you to pick pain," Alex said over the phone line. "He wouldn't want to be responsible for another man's death even if it might mean his own."

"Alex is right." I typed in the word *pain* and waited. The next several seconds were some of the longest of my life. I felt a trail of sweat crawl down my back, but I was too nervous to move or even breathe. Eventually, the phone rang. I answered it. As before, the message was recorded. *"Congratulations. You have passed and have earned the right to move on to the next challenge. If you complete it you will be at the halfway point. The next clue can be found where paupers rest. You have one hour."*

I let out a long breath of relief. I hoped the electrical shock wasn't too painful, but at least Zak and Fred were still alive. If there even was a Fred. "Do you think there even is a Fred and Wilma?" I asked.

"Probably not," Diego answered. "Though there's no way to know for sure. My feeling is, if you'd answered *Zak* he would have died. Risking his life to ensure that the other man didn't die was really your only move."

"It would have been nice if you'd said as much before I chose."

"Hey," Diego defended himself, "I didn't want to be responsible for the choice any more than Mr. Denton did."

I guess I understood that. In his position I wouldn't want to be responsible either. "Okay, moving on. The next clue is where paupers rest. Any ideas?"

"My first instinct is a paupers' cemetery," Hazel said.

"Do you know where I might find such a place?"

Hazel looked uncertain. "We could research it, but we only have an hour to locate the cemetery, drive there, and find the clue.

"We need Ethan," Hazel and I said at the same time.

Hazel called Ethan Carlton, a retired history professor and part-time teacher at Zimmerman Academy, and explained the situation. There were two cemeteries nearby, he said, where, historically, those who couldn't afford a proper burial were laid to rest. One had been used prior to 1950; the other was used after Ashton Falls was redeveloped. The older cemetery was closest to the library, so Levi, Hazel, and I would head there, and Ethan would call Phyllis and they would head over to the other one. We'd communicate by cell. Hopefully, we'd find whatever it was the madman behind this game wanted me to find. I sure hoped whoever had kidnapped Zak didn't mind that I had help because suddenly I had a whole team working with me.

I leaned my head against the back of the car seat as Levi drove quickly toward the cemetery. God, I was tired. I hoped if the next little mind game was the halfway point we'd actually finish today and Zak wouldn't have to spend another night wherever he was. I'd asked Hazel, who was my grandfather's girlfriend, not to mention any of this to him until it was over. I knew he'd worry and there was really nothing he could do to help. My parents had taken my little sister to Switzerland to visit my mother's family, so as long as Grandpa didn't know what was going on, there was no reason for them to find out either.

Hazel volunteered to call Salinger and fill him in on the status of my nightmare, and I closed my eyes and tried to imagine a happier time. My mind drifted over moments from the last few months. I'd known Zak would be a good father to any children we might have; what I hadn't known before Catherine arrived was how much my love for him would expand each time I caught him rocking Catherine in the middle of the night to avoid disturbing me, or making funny faces and silly voices when he changed her so she would smile at him with her tiny pink lips and huge blue eyes. I'd always known Zak was a loving, caring man, but since Catherine had come into our lives I'd had a glimpse of his uncertain, vulnerable side as well.

"It's just up ahead," Levi said, interrupting my daydream. "Any idea what to look for?"

"I guess an envelope and a cell. That's basically what we've found at the other sites, although the note at the library was in a book, not an envelope." I turned slightly to look at Hazel, who was sitting in the backseat. "Did Salinger have anything to say?"

"Not a lot. The medical examiner confirmed that Will was unconscious when he was shot. He was given an injection of an anesthetic drug that would have rendered him unconscious for at least an hour, possibly even longer."

"So why knock him out and then shoot him?" I asked. "It makes no sense." I groaned in frustration and closed my eyes once again. Damn, I hated this.

"You told me that Salinger found Will's body after someone called 911 and reported hearing a gunshot. He arrived at the motel and found Will dead on the floor of his room with the note and cell phone in his hands. He called Levi and had him fetch you," Hazel said.

"Yes. That's right."

"If Will hadn't been shot nothing would have been heard and there wouldn't have been a 911 call. Salinger wouldn't have responded and he wouldn't have called Levi and asked him to bring you to the motel."

"Yeah. So?"

"So if Will hadn't been shot, how would the game have gotten started?"

I opened my eyes and sat straight up. "I guess it would have started when Will woke up and found the note and phone. I suppose he would have called me."

"So why shoot Will?" Hazel asked the question we all had. "And if the plan was to shoot him all along why bother with drugging him first?"

I let out an exhausted groan. "I don't know. All we're doing is talking in circles. None of this makes sense."

Levi pulled onto the side of the road when we arrived at the old cemetery. We piled out and looked around at the grounds, which were overgrown with weeds and shrubs. There were no headstones to identify the person buried in each plot, though there had at one point been more crudely fashioned wooden crosses than now remained.

I stood at the edge of the cemetery and looked around. If whoever had Zak had hidden the phone and instructions here, they would most likely have found a place to leave them that was sheltered from the weather. It hadn't snowed in the past couple of days, but there were still patches of snow on the ground.

I took out my cell and called Ethan. "Are you there?"

"We are. So far we haven't found anything. Of course, we don't know exactly what we're looking for."

"Every clue so far has been provided in the form of a note and a cell phone. Are there any structures where you are? Crypts perhaps?"

"No. This was a pauper's cemetery. All that's left are a few wooden crosses. It was last used in 1970. I believe the cemetery where you are was abandoned by the late 1940s. Do you see any freshly dug graves?"

I scanned the area with my eyes. If the graveyard hadn't been used in almost seventy years freshly turned ground would be suspect. "No, but I do see a cross that looks a lot newer than the others." I walked over to it. It was fashioned with aged wood so as not to be too obvious, but it was screwed together rather than being nailed. "I think I found something."

I knelt and looked carefully at the ground near the cross. It didn't appear as if it had been disturbed for a very long time. There weren't any words on the cross, but one end of the bar had been carved to a pointed tip. I got down low to the ground and lined my eyes up in the direction the bar pointed toward. There was a tree about twenty yards away. I got up and walked to it. There was a small hole in the trunk of the tree that opened to a hollow center. The hole wasn't large enough to make out what was inside, so I held my breath and stuck my hand inside, hoping the tree wasn't the residence of a squirrel or some other woodland creature who might attack any intruder who dared interrupt his winter nap.

"I think I feel something." I handed the phone to Hazel, who was standing beside me.

"Be careful," Levi said. "There's no telling what might be sleeping inside the trunk of that tree."

I wrapped my fingers around something that felt like an envelope and slowly pulled it out. Inside was a note, another thumb drive, and another burner cell.

I unfolded the note and read it. *The phone will ring at nine twenty-five. When it does provide the answer to the following question: Fifty years ago Leo hammered a nail into this tree to mark his height. If the tree grew by five centimeters each year, how many inches higher would the nail be now?*

"More math," I groaned.

"Calling Alex right now," Levi replied.

Alex answered on the first ring. I read her the riddle.

"The nail wouldn't be any higher," Alex said. "Trees grow thicker at the bottom, but they only grow in height from their tops."

I frowned. "Really? How do you know all this stuff?"

"Genius. Remember?"

I guess I knew that intellectually, but the girl still never ceased to amaze me. Just to be sure, Levi Googled "tree growth" and found she was correct. We all decided that when the phone rang my answer would be that the nail would be zero inches farther up the tree, and it was fine. The voice on the other end of the phone said I would find the fifth challenge by deciphering the thumb drive in the envelope.

I told Alex we were coming with another thumb drive. She and Diego promised to be ready to meet whatever challenge the wacko who had Zak could throw at them.

Chapter 4

When Hazel, Levi, and I showed up at the house, Phyllis and Ethan were waiting for us. Alex met me at the front door and I handed off the thumb drive. Ellie, who was waiting right behind her with Catherine in her arms, handed me my daughter, who I was thrilled to see, and then shepherded everyone into the kitchen. The countertop was covered with various brunch items. Ellie instructed everyone to eat to fuel up for the day ahead, while I headed upstairs to spend some time with my baby. When I entered Zak and my bedroom with Charlie on my heels and Catherine in my arms, I found the gas fireplace had been clicked on, there was a comfy throw on the sofa in front of the fireplace, and a tray with coffee, juice, and assorted breakfast foods was waiting for me on the coffee table. Leave it to Ellie to know exactly what I needed. I was so grateful to my friends for their help, but I needed a few minutes of peace and quiet to still the screaming in my head.

Catherine seemed to be in a good mood, which helped a lot. Ellie had bathed, fed, and changed her, so she was content to lay on the sofa next to me, waving her arms and kicking her legs and squealing in delight every time Charlie, who was laying nearby, gently put a paw on her stomach. I smiled despite the terror I was feeling. The tasks I'd been asked to do so far had been varied. Some, like the game theory challenge, had been emotionally draining, while others, like the mathematical equations, had been intellectually challenging. I supposed whoever was behind this madness was counting on me getting help. Unless this person didn't know me at all, they should have had no expectation I could accomplish everything I'd been asked to do on my own.

I knew I should try to eat something, even though the very thought of food made me want to heave. Ellie had been correct: If we were to see this through we would need our strength. I took a sip of coffee and then nibbled the corner of an apple slice. Someone would come to get me once Alex had something to share, so I tucked Catherine between my body and the back of the sofa and stretched out beside her. Charlie curled into the crook made by my bent legs as I settled into a fetal position and slipped off into a void for a few precious moments.

I probably only slept for a short time, maybe fifteen minutes, but when I woke Catherine was asleep. I carefully transferred her into her own bed, then went into the bathroom, splashed water on my face, then headed downstairs to see how Alex was doing. When I entered the computer room I found her and Diego sitting side by side and whispering. This was a random thought to have at such a time, but I couldn't help but notice that Alex's long dark hair was almost the same color as Diego's shorter but much thicker hair.

"Did you get in?" I asked.

Alex turned and looked at me. She frowned. "Yes."

"And…?"

"And the instructions are to hack into the NSA and create a back door."

I leaned against the wall behind me. "Can you do that?"

Alex shook her head. "No. Not without help. Zak could probably do it, but we obviously can't enlist his help. I thought about calling Pi." She'd referred to Zak's ward, who was now a college student and junior partner in Zak's cyber security company.

Diego had a frown on his face. He took a moment before he spoke. "What I think we need to ask ourselves isn't so much *can we do it* as *should we do it?*"

I paused as I let this sink in. My first reaction was that we should definitely do it. Zak's life was at stake. But we were, after all, talking about national security. There was no telling why the person who was holding Zak wanted that back door, but I was pretty sure it wasn't because they were planning a surprise party. Or maybe they were, if you didn't take the word *party* too literally.

"What should we do, Zoe?" Alex asked.

"How much time do we have left?"

Alex looked at the clock. "About three hours."

I walked across the room and sat down on the sofa. I put my elbows on my knees and rested my head in my hands. Zak wouldn't want us to do anything that might threaten national security even if it meant his death. But there was no damn way I was just going to sit back and let the love of my life slip out of my hands.

"Zoe?" Alex asked again.

I lifted my head and found them looking at me. I thought back to the game theory test we'd dealt with earlier. When faced with an impossible situation the only thing to do was cheat. "I have an idea." I explained, and when she agreed we put it into action.

I hadn't so much come up with a plan as a plea for help. I called the one man I thought could know what to do in this situation. Everyone called him Shredder, which I was sure wasn't his real name. He was some sort of high-level government spy or black ops team member or something. I wasn't clear on exactly what he did, but based on the two occasions we'd spent time together, he not only had mad hacker skills but had contacts in the highest level of the military and government.

I explained what was going on and Shredder agreed to help Alex set up a back door they could access, but if anyone else did an alarm would be set off that Shredder would be monitoring. It took Alex. Shredder, and Diego most of the three hours we had to put the plan into action. It would have taken longer if Shredder didn't already have clearance to access the NSA site, which once again made me wonder if whoever had Zak didn't know exactly what sort of resources I had at my disposal.

Alex had just finished when the latest burner cell dinged. The text instructed me to send a link to the back door to a specific IP address. Once Alex had done that we waited for the next set of instructions. Luckily, it didn't take long to receive them.

You have passed the fifth test. The sixth will bring you one step closer to seeing your husband. You are to access the NSA through the back door you have created and obtain a file. The file will be labeled Chameleon. *Once you have the file you are to download it and send it to me. You have one hour.*

I looked at Alex and Diego, both of whom had frowns on their faces. "What do I do?" I asked Shredder, who was still on speakerphone.

"Give me five minutes to look into this and I'll call you back." He hung up.

I knew five minutes was going to seem like an eternity. Ellie, Levi, Phyllis, Ethan, and Hazel had joined us. No one spoke. I was sure no one knew what to say. Zak wouldn't want me to steal a file that might threaten national security, but I couldn't let him die. I just hoped Shredder could come up with a solution.

It took Shredder less than five minutes to call me back. I put him on speaker again.

"The file is a compilation of data gathered on a fugitive who's wanted internationally and recently escaped from a federal prison," Shredder informed me.

"Who?" I asked.

"Her name is Claudia Lotherman. She's not only a master of disguise but as slippery as an eel. It took years to track her down and capture her, and now she's managed to slip out of federal custody."

"I know Claudia," I said as a weight that felt like a ton settled in my stomach. "She's tried to kill me twice: once in Moosehead, Alaska, and once right here in Ashton Falls."

"Explain."

I closed my eyes as I tried to picture the woman who really could look like anyone. "The first time I crossed paths with Claudia she was pretending to be an old woman named Ethel Montros. She was staying at the same inn Zak and I were while we were in Moosehead to deliver a search-and-rescue dog to the local team. During our stay, Claudia killed a man named Colin Michaels, who was also staying at the inn. Apparently, he'd been tracking Claudia for quite some time. I'm not sure how long, but I found a whole lot of photos from all over the world in his room. Anyway, he'd tracked her to the inn in Alaska. Somehow, she found out what he was doing and killed him. Zak and I'd tried to figure out who the killer was, but all our theories met with dead ends. Then I accidentally figured out that the old woman who seemed too frail to have killed anyone wasn't old at all. I realized she had to be the killer because we'd eliminated everyone else. When I foolishly confronted her, she tried to kill me, but I got away by jumping from a moving car into an icy lake and swimming to freedom."

I took a deep breath before I continued. "The second time Claudia and I came into contact was right here in Ashton Falls. She was disguised as a man named Longines Walters. He was one of the team members my mother-in-law hired for Zak and my wedding and was staying in our home." I felt my stomach knot as I remembered that very difficult time in my life. "Walters was a very large, flamboyant man who was there to make sure I was camera-ready for all the events Zak's mom had planned."

"How did you find out Walters was Claudia?" Shredder asked.

"He—or I guess I should say she—killed a woman named Julianna, who was also staying in our house. After an investigation that seemed to be getting me nowhere I stumbled on to Longines without his padding or makeup, snooping in Zak's office. I realized right away it was Claudia. She wanted a file that was in Zak's safe and kidnapped me to force Zak to bring it to her. Once Zak brought the file to her, she tied us up and left us to die in an old mine shaft. Levi and Ellie saved us and the local sheriff caught up with her and turned her over to the FBI." I felt my voice catch. "If Claudia has Zak she'll kill him."

"We don't know for certain Claudia has Zak," Shredder reminded me. "We just know the person who has Zak wants Claudia's file."

"Can we give it to them?"

"Yes," Shredder assured me. "I changed a couple of facts regarding our current search for her that shouldn't be noticed and might actually help us track her down if she's the one asking for the file. Have Alex go in as instructed. Someone may be watching. Have her access the file, copy it, and send it to the kidnapper as requested. I'll stay on the line and walk her through it."

I handed the phone to Alex, who got to work. I just hoped this whole thing would be over soon. I felt my physical and emotional strength waning. I wasn't sure how much longer I could continue without having a complete and total breakdown. I looked at the faces of those standing around me and realized I wasn't alone in my journey through hell. Zak had touched the lives of everyone in the room, and there wasn't a soul among us who wasn't praying there would be a way to bring Zak home safely at the end of the road.

Once Shredder had helped Alex access and copy the file he rang off, but not before promising to call back for an update. He hoped once Claudia had the file, she'd use the information to make her way into the trap he'd prepared. He had matters to put into place and wanted to be ready.

Although we had the file ready early, we decided to wait until the last minute to send it. We didn't want the person at the end of the line to get suspicious if Alex finished more quickly than had been anticipated. Whoever was behind the game would most likely assume we'd enlist Pi's help, if he didn't know about Shredder. With Pi's assistance, it would have been difficult to get the file in time; we certainly wouldn't have finished early.

When the deadline was less than a minute away Alex sent the file. Then we waited for a call or text outlining the next task. By my calculations, there were only two left. I wanted this over with and Zak home where he should be. I just hoped Claudia, or whoever had wanted her file, would release him, as had been promised.

A minute later, I received a text: *Alex and Pi have done well. The phone will ring in two minutes with your next set of instructions.*

It terrified me that this wacko had Alex and Pi's names and knew who I would go to for help. Of course, Pi hadn't actually helped, but it was better they not know about Shredder. If they did they may have questioned the authenticity of the file. Still, that the person who'd killed Will and kidnapped Zak knew about Alex and Pi scared the living daylights out of me. I just hoped I hadn't put them in danger by playing along with them.

When the phone rang I answered. As before, there was a computer-generated message: *The instructions for the next task will be found at Wilbur's Folly. You have two hours to find them and complete the task.*

"Wilbur's Folly?" Phyllis asked.

"Wilbur's Folly is a mine," Hazel explained. "Back when this area was known as Devil's Den, Wilbur Fortnight came here with a fortune he'd inherited from his grandfather. He didn't need the money mining might bring, but he had the fever and was determined to find his share of the gold rumored to be found here. The other miners knew he was wealthy, so they came up with a plot to make him think he'd found a rich vein when all he'd really found was dirt. They planted gold in his mine and sold him the equipment he'd need to excavate at ten times the usual rate. In the end he died a broke and broken man and the men who'd tricked him had his fortune."

"That was really mean," Alex said.

"It was," I agreed. "It will take us a good forty minutes to get up to the mine." I looked at Levi. "Are you ready?"

"Two steps ahead of you."

"We'll follow in Ethan's car," Phyllis said.

I reminded Alex and Diego once again not to leave the house but to wait by the phone. I joined Levi in his vehicle while Hazel, Phyllis, and Ethan followed behind. The mine was at the end of a dirt road that wound its way up the mountain. We'd have to park at the end of the road and continue up the mountain on foot to the entrance to the mine shaft. Levi and I were young and in good shape, but the three seniors weren't quite as well equipped to make the hike, so they'd wait by the cars for us to return with the instructions.

"Why on earth would they put clues all the way up here?" I asked as Levi and I climbed the steep trail. We were both in good shape, but that didn't prevent us from breathing heavily.

Levi gasped for air. "It seems like an odd place to hide a clue. Although maybe this task speaks to the physical part of the challenge. So far, the tests have challenged you in an emotional and intellectual way, but none have been physically difficult."

"I suppose that could be true. I just hope we find the clues in time. It took a long time to get here and this hike isn't easy."

"We'll make it," Levi assured me as we picked up the pace despite our fatigue.

In spots the climb was almost straight up and my legs and lungs were burning by the time we reached the opening to the mine shaft. I hoped the envelope would be sitting there in plain sight, but I could picture the devil behind this plot wasn't going to make it easy.

"I guess we need to go inside," Levi said.

I really, really didn't want to go inside the dark, narrow passage, but I didn't think we had much of a choice.

"I'll go in," I said. "You wait here in case I get into trouble. I may need you to rescue me again."

"No, I'll go in and you wait," Levi said.

I shook my head. "This game is directed at me. I need to be the one to go. I won't be able to text or call once I get inside; if I'm not back in ten minutes assume I need help."

Levi didn't look thrilled with my plan, but he didn't argue. I used the flashlight on my phone and gingerly took a step into the cold, dark shaft. The farther from the entrance I got the more claustrophobic I began to feel. The ceiling became increasingly lower, the walls seeming to close in on each other. I took several deep breaths to even my breathing. Hyperventilating and passing out weren't an option. The clock was ticking. I needed to find the envelope and find it fast.

When I came to a spot that looked to have suffered a cave-in I paused. To continue, I would need to lay down and squeeze through on my belly. I had no idea how far I would have to crawl before I could stand up again. I turned and looked back toward the entrance. I could barely see the light, but I could still feel fresh air. I looked back toward the low space. Had whoever left the clues come into the shaft this far? Maybe I'd missed it, or it wasn't inside the cave at all. Should I go back or should I continue?

I was frozen with indecision. If the clues were on the other side and I didn't go on I wouldn't have the information I needed to finish the game and Zak would die. If I went on and the shaft caved in on me, I wouldn't finish the game and Zak would still die. If I went on and lived but didn't find the clue, I might not have the time to get back through and look in another location, and Zak would die. Time was running out. I needed to make a decision.

If Claudia was the one behind this she very well could have hidden the clue on the other side. She was a tall, thin woman who I was sure could slip through the space that would be much too small for someone as large as Levi to navigate. The person behind the game had directed it at me. Maybe the small space was the designer's way of ensuring I would be the one to retrieve the package.

Making a decision, I lay down on my stomach and began to pull my body forward along the cold, hard floor. I could feel the walls brushing my back and both sides. If I were a few pounds heavier I would have been stuck for sure. The farther I traveled into the tight space, the more I felt my panic build. Had I made the right choice? Would I make it to the other side or become stuck along the way? The worst part was that I couldn't see much in the darkness and had no idea how long I would need to endure the tight space. My heart pounded, my breath quickened, and sweat trickled down my face and into my eyes despite the cool dampness of the mine. I blinked my eyes to clear the sweat, but it did no good. My arms were in front of me pulling me forward, slowly but steadily. It was too tight to bring them back to wipe my face, so I simply endured. Just when I thought I was going to give in to my panic and scream I felt an open space in front of me. I let out a long breath, then took a deep breath in. I pulled myself forward at a faster pace, anxious to feel the emptiness of space around me.

Once I climbed out I took a moment to wipe my face with my arm before looking around for the envelope. I let out a breath of relief when I saw the envelope waiting in plain sight. I wanted to take a moment to calm my nerves, but I was running out of time, so I picked up the envelope and tucked it beneath my shirt. I moved it around until it was between my shirt and my back and then got back down on my stomach again. I just hoped the extra bulk wouldn't end up getting me stuck. It seemed that might happen, but I needed my hands to pull myself back through, so holding the envelope wasn't an option.

It was easier going out. For one thing, the risks involved in not knowing what I was getting in to and whether I'd become stuck without even finding the envelope had been eliminated. And the knowledge that there was an open area waiting for me gave me the courage to navigate the tight space without feeling the panic I had on my way in.

When I reached the spot where I could stand up and move around, I took the envelope out and hurried forward. I was just exiting the mine when my phone rang. If it had rung a few seconds earlier I wouldn't have had reception and the whole task could most likely have been considered a failure.

"Hello," I said as I paused next to Levi.

As before, there was a computer-generated message. *"You have passed the seventh task by conquering your fear and doing what needed to be done. Only one task left. This one won't be quite so easy. There is an abandoned warehouse at the very end of the old logging road on the north end of town. Enter the warehouse and await further instructions. You may bring one friend. Choose wisely. You have thirty minutes to reach the warehouse and answer the phone, which you will find in the center of the room."*

I looked at Levi. "We need to head to the old logging road on the north end of town. I'll fill you in on the way."

Fortunately, the hike down the trail was quicker than the one up. When we reached the others Hazel gasped and Phyllis put a hand to her mouth. "What happened?" Ethan asked.

I realized I must look a fright. Between the sweat and the dirt, I probably had mud on my face, and my clothes and hair must be a mess.

"I don't have time to explain. We're heading to a warehouse at the end of the old logging road on the north end of town. We have to hurry." I ran as fast as I could to Levi's car without waiting for a response.

Once we were underway, Levi broke every speed limit we encountered. Thankfully, we didn't have to travel through the busiest part of town on our way to the logging road. As Levi drove, I briefly told him about the narrow space I'd had to crawl though while I tried to decide who to bring into the warehouse with me. My instinct was to go alone. I realized this last test could very well be dangerous, and I didn't want to put any of my friends in danger. But the voice had said I could bring a friend, and it would be just my luck if I went in alone and then find out part of the task I had to perform was to flip two switches simultaneously on opposite sides of the room.

I wondered if I'd have time to enter alone, check out the situation, and then go back out and get one of my friends if another person was necessary. I sort of doubted it. Chances were, once I was inside the door would lock from the outside until the task was completed.

I wished I knew what would be required of me and whether I'd have cell service. If the task was physical I'd definitely want Levi with me, but he was the friend I least wanted to take along. Levi was a young man with a wife and a baby. He had a lot of life left to live and I didn't see how I could put him in what very well could be a life-threatening situation. Not that I would take the death of one of my three older friends lightly. But if Levi died... I couldn't let myself think about that.

I carefully considered each of my friends as analytically as I could. Ethan was intelligent and knew a lot about history, including the history of the area. He wasn't as strong as Levi by any stretch of the imagination, but he was probably stronger than either Phyllis or Hazel. If the tasks were intellectual rather than physical, any of the other three would be a better choice than Levi, but Ethan had a depth of knowledge I'd long admired. He was a single older man, so his death, if that was the inevitable end to this little game, would be felt less acutely than Levi's.

Phyllis was also single and knew a lot about literature, and Hazel had a lot of general knowledge from working in a library, but she was my grandfather's girlfriend. Of course, if intellect was needed for the challenge, Alex or Diego would be the best choice by far, but there was no way I was getting them involved, no matter what was at stake.

I sighed as we neared our destination. Logic wasn't going to cut it. There was no way I was going to be able to ask any of my friends to come with me when the situation we would be walking into was so completely unknown. But if two people were required to complete the task and I went in alone, Zak would die.

I closed my eyes and prayed for an answer. What should I do? Go in alone or ask a friend? If so, which friend? The voice had said no cops, which was unfortunate, because Salinger was the friend I would ask if that were an option.

"What's on your mind?" Levi asked. He must have noticed the struggle I'd been dealing with. I hadn't put the phone on speaker, so he hadn't heard the message and therefore didn't know about the decision I had to make.

"I'm just freaking out a bit. Now that we're on the last task I'm both relieved and terrified."

"I know what you mean. I feel the same way. I want this to be over, but if we fail…"

I leaned my head back against the seat. "I can't let myself think about that or I'll end up catatonic, which would render me unable to finish." I lifted my head. "Do you think there'll be cell service in the warehouse?"

Levi twisted his lips in a thoughtful manner. "Probably, unless the reception has been jammed. Open the glove box."

I did as he said and found two handheld radios.

"These are only good at close range. I use them to communicate with my assistant coaches during football games and practices. But if the phone signal is jammed these should work. We'll take one inside with us and Ethan, Hazel, and Phyllis can wait on the outside with the other one. That way we can access their knowledge base if we need it without putting them in any danger."

"That's a good idea, but I don't want you to be in any danger either. I should go in alone."

Levi shook his head. "Not going to happen. I'm coming, and unless you can overpower me there isn't a thing you can do about it."

"The last task very likely will be dangerous," I argued. "You have a wife and a child. You need to keep to the sidelines, out of harm's way."

Levi turned and glanced at me. The look on his face was hard and unyielding. "I'm not letting you do this alone. I understand your concern and would probably be saying the same thing to you if our roles were reversed. But I love you and Ellie loves you, and neither of us would choose for you to go in alone even knowing the risk."

I knew Levi was right and I really might need his help, but I'd never be able to live with myself if I ended up getting him killed. Of course, if that was the outcome I'd probably be dead as well, so I wouldn't have to live with the guilt for all that long. I thought of Ellie. She would suffer so much if something happened to Levi. And the thought of Eli growing up without a father was more than I could bear. Maybe I could sneak into the warehouse before Levi realized what I was doing. If the door did lock behind me, Levi would be unable to get in. Yes, I decided, that would be my plan. It was the only one I could live with.

Levi must have anticipated as much because when we arrived at the warehouse he grabbed my hand. "We go in together."

"But…"

"There is no but. If I have to drag you into the warehouse I will, but we're going together."

I nodded. I wanted to argue, but suddenly I felt too weak to even speak. Levi helped me out of the car. He released his grip on me but kept me within arm's reach. He gave one of the handheld radios to Ethan and explained the plan. No one mentioned the danger or the possibility that this was a trap and Levi, Zak, and I would all die.

Levi took my hand and led me into the large, windowless warehouse. The door clicked shut behind us in such a way that there was no reason to wonder whether we were locked in.

"Showtime," Levi said as he headed toward the middle of the room, where the burner cell awaited our arrival.

Chapter 5

Levi and I waited for the phone to ring. The walls were tall, at least fifteen feet, and made of cinderblock. The roof looked to be made from some sort of aluminum, which might theoretically be possible to cut through, if you had a way to get to the roof and the right tool to do the cutting. Inside the warehouse were various items, including old furniture, artwork on the walls, and a variety of devices that looked a lot like ancient torture devices. The oddest item in the room was a giant screen that took up almost an entire wall. I wondered if the game master wasn't finally going to make him or herself known.

Despite knowing the phone was going to ring, and that I'd been waiting for that very thing to happen, I jumped when it did. I picked it up after the first ring and pressed the Answer button. At the exact moment I did, the screen on the wall came on. I put my hand to my mouth as tears streamed down my cheeks. On the screen was the image of Zak tied up and sitting in a chair. It looked like we were viewing the room where he was being held in real time, so at least we knew he was alive.

"Zak," I called. "Can you hear me?"

Zak didn't respond in any way, so I doubted he could hear or even knew I could see him. I had no idea where he was and didn't like the object, which looked a lot like a bomb, sitting on a table next to him. I held the phone to my ear and listened.

"Welcome to the locked room. As you can see, your husband is alive and well. The image you are seeing is in real time. However this ends, I wanted you to be able to see the love of your life one last time. The final game is simple. The object you see on the table next to Zak is a bomb. If it goes off it will destroy the building, killing him instantly. The bomb has been set up with a computer-operated Off switch. You will be given four tasks. Each one you complete will be communicated via the computer in the warehouse to the computer monitoring the bomb. If you complete all four tasks before the timer runs out the bomb will be deactivated and you will be given the location where Zak is being held. If you fail to complete the tasks in the time allotted, the bomb will be go off and you will watch your husband die. From the time this call ends you will have two hours to do everything to save your husband."

The phone went dead. Levi looked at his cell. "There's no reception. I'm setting my timer for one hour and fifty minutes. There's no way I want this to come down to the wire."

"Oh God," was my only response as I stood frozen, looking at Zak on the screen. My heart was slowly bleeding and I knew it wouldn't be long before I would no longer be able to maintain what little sanity I had left.

Levi grabbed me by the shoulders. He turned me so I was facing away from the screen. He looked me in the eye. "We don't have time for a breakdown. Do you understand? You need to pull yourself together."

I nodded because I still couldn't speak.

"The door is locked and the clock is ticking. We need to act quickly and efficiently."

"But Zak…" I tried to turn my head.

"Don't look at Zak. Look at me."

I did as Levi instructed.

"You have to get it together. If you don't Zak will die."

I took a long, slow breath. "Okay. You're right. Where do we start?"

Levi tried the radio, which worked. He briefly told the others what was going on. He described the room in which Zak was being held to the best of his ability and then instructed them to call Salinger to fill him in and then stand by. Then he looked around. "It's odd they didn't tell us where to find the instructions for the first task."

I looked around as well. I wasn't sure if the tasks needed to be completed in a specific order. The voice on the phone hadn't said. I scanned the room slowly and methodically. There were a lot of things in the room. The instructions could be anywhere. I noticed a metal box that looked a lot like a makeup kit. "There." I pointed to it. If Claudia was behind this the makeup box would be as quintessential a clue as there was likely to be. Luckily, I was correct. Inside the box was makeup and a sheet of paper.

"How'd you know where to look?" Levi asked.

"Knowing it's probably Claudia behind this provided the clue I needed. Where better to leave a clue than a makeup box when you're a master of disguise?"

"Good thinking. What does it say?"

"'Find the sailor's trunk and open the lid. Take out the game controller and press the green button.'"

Levi and I headed in separate directions, frantically looking for the sailor's trunk. I tried to stay focused, but I couldn't help but be acutely aware that with every minute that passed Zak was one minute closer to death.

"I found it," I shouted as I opened the lid of the trunk and took out the controller. I pressed the green button and a message popped up on the screen where Zak's image had been.

Levi read it out loud. "'In ten seconds a video game will replace this message on the screen. If you can beat the game in twenty minutes or less you will have completed one of the tasks required. If your character in the game dies at any point or you fail to finish within twenty minutes, Zak dies." Levi never looked away from the screen, but he did reach over and take the controller from me. "Set the timer on your phone for twenty minutes."

As I slipped my phone out of my pocket, a game appeared on the screen. It was one Zak had developed. He'd showed me the object of the game and shared with me some strategy to beat it, but my character usually ended up dying in the first sixty seconds. As I watched Levi's thumbs work the controller with steady accuracy, I knew for the first time since we'd been locked in the room that choosing Levi as my one friend had been the right decision. Not that I chose Levi exactly. It was more that he chose me. But I was pretty sure not one of the seniors waiting outside had every played the game, and I knew without a doubt I would never have made it to the end.

I wanted to ask Levi how he was doing, but I didn't want to break his concentration, so I simply stood and watched him, all the while fighting the feeling of dread in my stomach. I cringed when his avatar suffered an injury. It could continue even with the injury, but he would have lost some of his weapons and would need to earn them back. I just hoped Levi had the time to do it.

He never took his eyes from the screen. He never spoke or even moved except for his thumbs on the controller. I wasn't familiar enough with the game to know if he was far enough along to make the twenty-minute deadline, but again, I didn't want to break his concentration, so I didn't ask.

When the timer on my phone revealed that fifteen minutes had passed I began to sweat. At the seventeen-minute mark my heart was pounding so hard in my chest that I could barely breathe. I wasn't particularly religious, but I found myself praying harder than I ever had before.

"How long?" Levi asked just as the second hand approached the nineteen-minute mark.

"You have one minute left."

Levi seemed to focus even harder. His thumbs moved even faster than they had before. I could see he was in the zone, so I kept quiet even as the second hand moved past the nineteen-minute and thirty-second mark. At nineteen minutes and forty seconds he stopped what he was doing.

"Are you done? Did you beat the game?"

Levi grinned. "Of course. I always win. I can even beat Zak a lot of the time."

I threw myself in his arms as the screen changed from the game to the next set of instructions. They were written beneath Zak's image, so I could see him and the bomb as well. I noticed that where there had been four little green lights on the bomb's casing before, now there were three green lights and one red. Apparently, we needed to turn all the lights red.

Levi began to speak as he read the words on the screen aloud. "'The instructions for your next task are taped to the ceiling. You have thirty minutes to retrieve them and complete the task.'"

I set my timer for thirty minutes and then looked up at the ceiling. "So how are we going to get them down?"

The ceiling was about fifteen feet in the air, so I knew we'd need to build a ladder of some sort. The problem was, there was nothing around other than the sailor's trunk that looked like it was both sturdy enough and shaped right for stacking.

Levi must have come to the same conclusion. "The trunk is about three feet high. I'm six feet tall and you're five feet. If I stand on the trunk and you stand on my shoulders you might be able to reach it."

While this was further confirmation Levi had been the right choice of friend—none of the seniors would be able to support my weight—I still had my doubts it would work.

I helped Levi pull the trunk under the envelope taped to the ceiling. He stood on it and then I carefully climbed onto his shoulders. I reached my hand over my head; I was about a foot short of reaching the ceiling.

"I can't reach it. We need to find something I can use to knock it free."

"No time," Levi said. "On the count of three, bend your legs, jump up, and grab the envelope. I'll catch you."

I hesitated for just a minute and did as Levi suggested. I figured even if he failed to catch me and I landed on the cement floor, I probably wouldn't die, but if we didn't complete the task in time Zak would. Luckily, I was able to grab the envelope and Levi caught me.

He set me down on the chest next to him and we both jumped down to the floor, where I opened the envelope. "'Go to the garment bag and find the keyboard. Type in the number that corresponds to the record of most completed passes by an NFL player in any single season.'"

I looked at Levi.

"Drew Brees set a record of 471 completions in 2016."

I looked around for a garment bag. There was so much stuff in the warehouse, finding any specific object was difficult.

"I found it," Levi said after a minute had passed. He took out the keyboard and typed in the answer. Once again, Zak's image disappeared from the screen and was replaced with a puzzle. This time it was a partially filled in Sudoku. The instructions said to use the arrows and keypad to fill in the rest of the numbers.

"I don't suppose you're a master at this game as well?" I asked hopefully.

Levi shook his head. "Sorry. Looks like you're up."

I took a deep breath and looked at the puzzle. I'd done these in the past and understood the basic idea. Every row and column, as well as each individual box, could only have one of any specific number, yet every number, one through nine, needed to be represented. The problem was, I was a beginner, or on a good day an intermediate player, but based on the scarcity of numbers shown on the screen, this puzzle was meant for an expert player.

I had little choice but to play, so I did. I took a cue from Levi and focused on the screen and the game. I had the feeling if I made one wrong move Zak would die. I had a few uncertain moments, but I was making steady progress. The problem was, unless things started to come together a bit more quickly, I was never going to make the deadline.

"Five minutes left," Levi said from beside me.

I was at the point where I knew if I could just get two or three more numbers everything would come together and I could fill out the rest without too much effort. But I was stuck. I'd looked at every open box a dozen times, but I could do no better than limit the options to two numbers for each box.

"Four minutes," Levi said after I had been staring at the puzzle for a good minute without making a move.

I didn't have time to go over everything again. The only option was to guess. I located the box where I felt I had the highest probability of guessing the right answer and typed in a three.

Nothing happened. The game didn't beep at me and Zak's image exploding didn't show on the screen. I must have guessed right. Filling in that one number gave me enough information to fill in the whole row, which gave me enough information to finish the puzzle with a whole minute left over. When the puzzle disappeared and was replaced with Zak's image, as well as words beneath it, I felt the knot in my stomach relax just a bit.

I immediately looked at the face of the bomb to find two red lights and two green.

Levi began to read. "'Go to the sailor's trunk. You will find a thick board with wires attached to it. The board will have two handles on each side. Plug the wire you find into the keyboard and then stand facing each other with the board between you. Your task is to level the board. When you do the light will turn green. Your task at that point is to keep the green light on for fifteen minutes. If the board isn't kept perfectly level a red light will come on. If that happens Zak dies. If you manage to keep the board perfectly level for the entire fifteen minutes a buzzer will sound to alert you that you have been successful.'"

Levi headed for the trunk, while I radioed the others. "We're being timed so we can't talk now. We're doing okay so far. Stand by."

"We're here if you need us," Ethan responded.

Levi retrieved the board and plugged it into the keyboard. A timer popped onto the screen. I imagined that was how long we had to get the board level in the first place. Levi and I stood facing each other, legs slightly apart to provide more stability. We each took the handles on our own side of the board and worked to get it level. It was harder than it sounded at first. Eventually, the green light appeared and we both froze. Even the slightest movement would move the little bubble in the center, killing Zak.

Two seconds after the green light went on my nose started to itch. I knew I couldn't remove a hand from the board to scratch it, so I tried to ignore it. My eyes met with Levi's. He didn't say anything and neither did I. I think we both knew the smallest distraction could be disastrous. We stood staring into each other's eyes for several minutes until I looked away.

Each minute seemed like an hour. The board was heavy and my arms started to scream when we were only about five minutes into the fifteen minutes we had to stay completely still. Once again, I was certain Levi had been the correct friend to help me. None of the seniors could have held the board for fifteen minutes. I wasn't even certain I could do it, but with Zak's life on the line I'd find a way.

I let my mind drift to thoughts of Zak while keeping part of my attention on the board. When Zak had first come back to Ashton Falls after making gazillion dollars developing computer software, I hadn't been happy at all. When Levi invited him to come along with him to a BBQ I was having at my boathouse I was downright livid. But over the next few weeks Zak did a lot of little things that forced me to like him. When he bought an empty building to renovate and turn into an animal shelter after I was fired from my animal control job with the county, I found myself starting to love him.

I found, once I opened my heart to him, that Zak was kind and funny and patient. He had a few quirks

I'd found amusing, like using a spreadsheet to choose the most cost-effective brand of laundry detergent, but as we spent time together and I was able to see the man he'd become, the man he'd most likely already been, I realized there was no one in the world I'd rather build a life with.

Of course, it still took me a ridiculous amount of time to say yes after he proposed to me. Three months, to be exact. And even longer to finally get myself to the altar after that. But looking back at everything Zak and I had been through, the good and the bad, I realized I wouldn't trade one minute of our time together for anything in the world.

My arm jerked when the buzzer sounded. I started to panic and immediately began to cry, but Levi grabbed my hand and told me the noise had been the timer letting us know we'd been successful.

I wrapped my arms around Levi's neck and sobbed anyway. He hugged me hard and took a step back. He looked me in the eye. "We have one more task."

"Okay," I said, taking a step back and wiping my eyes with my arm.

The image of Zak was back on the screen, and once again there were words beneath his image. The face of the bomb now had three red lights and one green.

Just one more to go.

Once again Levi began to read. "'You may have noticed that Zak hasn't moved since this little game began. He was told the bomb was equipped with a motion detector. Think of how difficult that last test was for you. Zak has been perfectly still for several hours. Let's just hope he can make it long enough for you to disarm the bomb by completing the final task.'"

I glanced at Zak. I could barely stand to see him this way. The knowledge that the bomb was equipped with a motion detector made me feel even more desperate.

"We need to hurry," I said. "What's next?"

Just as I said that, an image popped up on the screen. It looked like an equation of some sort, showing rows of Ys and Os, with one X. Each Y and O had a number next to it. The instructions were to define X.

"Crap," Levi said aloud. "Should we call the others and have them call Alex?"

I was about to agree with Levi when I noticed there was a number in the lower left corner, counting down from 200.

"We don't have time." I looked Levi in the eye. "Look closely at the board. Does it look familiar?"

"You know I suck at math."

"The original message I received said I could bring one friend into the warehouse with me. I wasn't sure at first which friend would be best, but I'm certain now the friend who could most help me and save Zak was you."

Levi looked doubtful.

"There's no one else who could have beat the video game in time. And neither Alex nor any of the seniors could have held me up so we could retrieve the envelope on the ceiling. And I'm certain no one beside you in my circle of friends know what the single season passing record was off the top of their head. This contest is about you and me working together. Now look at the screen and tell me how to define X."

Levi looked back at the screen. He appeared to be terrified, but he also seemed determined. I could see Zak's image in the background as Levi studied the numbers and letters on the screen. I glanced at the timer. Only fifty seconds left. *Come on, Levi. You can do this!*

"If I'm supposed to solve this, we have to assume this isn't a mathematical equation," Levi said.

Forty seconds.

"The numbers could be a clue, but I feel like they've been added to the letters to provide a distraction," Levi added.

Thirty seconds.

"If you take away the numbers it looks like a football play." Levi looked at me with twenty seconds left. "X is the quarterback."

I had no idea if he was right, but we only had twenty seconds left on the timer in the corner of the screen, so I quickly typed *X=Quarterback* on the keyboard.

The timer stopped and the equation disappeared from the screen. I glanced at the bomb. Four red lights.

"We did it." I raised my hand in the air.

"I hope so. The two-hour timer we were originally given has ten minutes left on it. Just to be safe we should get Zak out of there in the next ten minutes."

An address flashed on the screen.

My heart sank. The address was a good fifteen minutes away, even if we ran every red light.

"Salinger," I said. "If he's in his office he's only ten minutes away from where Zak is being held." I ran to the door and prayed it would open. It did. I stepped out and used my cell, which now worked, to make the call, while Levi tried to answer the questions the others were asking.

"Was he in his office?" Levi asked when I hung up.

"Better. He was out trying to find Zak after the seniors called him. He said he's only two minutes away from the address that flashed on the screen. Let's go."

Levi and I ran to his vehicle while the others piled into Ethan's car. Even though I was certain Salinger would beat us to Zak's location by quite a bit, Levi put the pedal to the metal. He ran every stop sign and red light, causing other cars to slam on their brakes. There was a lot of honking and I was sure a lot of cussing, but it didn't look like we'd caused any accidents. When we arrived at the abandoned building I jumped out of the car before Levi even came to a complete stop. I ran toward the building not knowing what I'd find. When I saw Zak sitting on a wall talking to Salinger I fell to my knees and sobbed.

Zak must have seen or heard me because he headed in my direction. He picked me up in his arms and held me close. We both sobbed until we had no more tears to shed.

Chapter 6

Tuesday, March 27

After everyone who'd been with us greeted Zak and expressed their relief that he was okay, we headed home, where everyone who was waiting there did the same. Neither of us had slept in forever, so once Zak made sure the kids were okay, we headed up to bed, where we fell immediately asleep in each other's arms.

Ellie and Levi had decided to stay at the house for the time being, but Levi drove Diego back to the dorm. Ellie must have continued to take care of Catherine because by the time I opened my eyes the sun was high in the sky. I reached for Zak, but his side of the bed was empty. I quickly washed up and got dressed, then went downstairs. I found him talking to Salinger. Both men were sitting at the kitchen table drinking coffee.

Zak opened his arms to me and I slid onto his lap. "What's up?" I asked as I wound one arm around his neck.

"We just needed to bring each other up to date," Salinger replied.

"We could have come in to your office if you needed information for your report."

"I'm not here about the report," Salinger said, glancing at Zak. They exchanged a look before anyone said another word.

I slipped off Zak's lap and onto a chair where I could better see his face. "What's going on?"

"Salinger and I were talking about Claudia and where she might have gone off to," Zak explained.

"I guess she must have gotten away," I said as I studied Zak's face. I could tell there was more, but I decided to wait for him to continue.

"Unfortunately, she did. In fact, she left right after you sent the file over from the NSA office. Everything that occurred after that was controlled by a preprogrammed computer."

Smart to have two time-consuming tasks after she made her escape to throw everyone off. "I'm sorry she escaped, but I suppose she's the feds problem now. Shredder added some false data to the file that he said should help them catch up with her."

"That was smart," Zak said. "But capturing Claudia isn't why Salinger is here. I called him and asked him to come over."

I furrowed my brow. I hadn't thought so. I prepared myself for something worse than a missing felon. "So what's going on?"

"Claudia didn't kill Will," Zak said.

"What? Are you sure?"

"Very sure." Zak nodded.

I groaned and momentarily closed my eyes. "So this isn't over."

"I'm afraid not." Zak put a hand on my leg. I opened my eyes and looked at him. He was exhausted. Totally spent. Did either of us have the strength to go on?

"Perhaps you should walk me through this," I said, fatigue evident in my voice.

Zak shifted in his chair. It appeared he was gearing up for a long conversation. I had no idea what he was going to say, but based on his expression I wasn't going to like it. "Claudia showed up at Will's motel room dressed as a pizza delivery driver. We'd ordered pizza so weren't suspicious. Claudia must have intercepted the call, or maybe she was outside the motel and saw him drive up. I'm not totally clear on that."

Zak ran a hand through his thick blond hair before he continued. His eyes were hollow and bloodshot. I knew how difficult this was for him. "Will opened the door and let her in. I didn't recognize her, mainly because she wasn't dressed as a woman. She looked like a young boy. Neither Will nor I suspected anything was off until she pulled a pizza box and a gun out of his delivery bag. Before I could respond, Claudia stabbed Will in the neck with a needle. He immediately fell to the ground. I feared he might be dead, but she assured me he wasn't. I had no idea it was Claudia I was dealing with yet, and to be honest I was so stunned I couldn't seem to move. After I had a chance to wrap my head around what had happened I demanded to know why this kid, who looked to be no more than a teenager, had killed Will. She told me that Will wasn't dead, only unconscious. Still holding the gun pointed to my head, she told me to put the phone and note, which were also in the pizza bag, in Will's hands. I was desperately trying to come up with a plan to gain the upper hand, but at least placing the items in Will's hands gave me the opportunity to verify for myself that he was breathing regularly. Other than the fact he was unconscious he seemed to be fine."

"And then…?" I prompted.

"The pizza delivery guy, who was surprisingly strong for his size, cuffed me and made me leave with him. He said we were going to play a little game and then I'd be free to go. He was holding all the cards, so I had little choice but to go along with him. I figured he wanted something from me and once I gave it to him the whole thing would be over."

"But it wasn't quite so easy," I said.

Zak shook his head. "We arrived at our destination and the kid left the room. When Claudia returned she'd changed out of her disguise and I realized who she really was. That's also when I realized I might be in real trouble. I still had no idea what Claudia wanted, but all I could do was take things as they came and try to deal with the situation as best I could. When she informed me that the game she intended to play was with you rather than me, I thought I would die. I wanted to do something to prevent you from going through what you did, but my hands were tied, literally. I can't even begin to explain the hell I went through watching her torture you."

"But you were okay? Physically?"

Zak nodded. "She didn't do anything to hurt me physically. In fact, she was very generous with food and water. Her game, it seemed, was a psychological one. She put you through hell, making you believe if you made one tiny mistake I would die, and she put me through hell, making me watch what she was doing to you."

"So she did have a camera on me?"

"Not all the time, but enough for me to see what her tests were doing to you."

My anger toward the woman who'd treated Zak and me like pawns in her sick, sick game was increasing by the minute. If I ever managed to get my hands on her, I'd... Well, I don't know what I'd do, but it would definitely include strong language.

"So the questions she asked and the documents she wanted access to—were they the reason for the test or was the test simply to entertain her?" I asked.

"I believe all she wanted was the file the NSA had on her. The rest was a smoke screen."

I thought about everything she'd asked me to do and realized Zak was probably correct. She needed the file for some reason and instead of just kidnapping Zak and forcing him to get it for her, she'd decided to have some fun at our expense.

"Okay, wait." I held up a hand as I suddenly realized I had become diverted from the real purpose of this conversation. "If Claudia didn't kill Will, who did?"

"We don't know," Salinger said.

Maybe somewhere along the way I'd actually lost my mind because this wasn't making a bit of sense. "Why would Claudia spare Will after she realized he was in her way? Even more to the point, why wouldn't she just wait until Zak was alone before she grabbed him? Was drugging Will part of her plan?"

"I don't know," Zak admitted. "I suppose she figured she could use Will as leverage to get me to cooperate, but it almost seemed as if she intentionally spared him."

"But Claudia likes to kill people," I pointed out. "She killed two people right under my nose. Why would she spare Will? Knocking him out doesn't seem to be her style at all."

Zak shrugged. "I'm sure nabbing me while I was with Will was a calculated move. Claudia doesn't seem the sort to be impulsive or careless. Perhaps she didn't know Will would die and planned to get him involved so he'd help you with the math required to complete the tasks. I'm sure she never planned for you to do it on your own."

"Not if she knows me at all," I mumbled.

"I don't think Claudia's intention, at least with this caper, was to harm or kill anyone. I think she simply wanted the file and found a way to have some fun with you at the same time."

I raised a brow. "What do you mean, she didn't plan to kill anyone? Don't forget she was within seconds of blowing you up."

"The bomb was a fake," Salinger said.

I wasn't sure if I was angry or relieved that Zak had never been in any real danger, which was a completely illogical thought to have. Of course I was relieved, but to think of the stress Levi and I had gone through when there was no real danger really pissed me off. "Fake? Are you sure?"

Salinger nodded.

When I thought of the hell Levi and I had gone through when we thought Zak might die I wanted to scream in frustration, although I didn't. I decided to refocus my attention on the matter at hand. "So the theory is that someone other than Claudia came into Will's room and shot him while he was unconscious?"

Zak nodded.

I rubbed a hand over my face and across my eyes. I needed a minute to process this. The odds that some random person unrelated to Claudia killed Will were just too astronomical to even consider. At least I imagined they were. As everyone knows, I really have no idea how to calculate the odds of anything. It did make sense that Claudia planned for Will to help me all along. She wouldn't have had any expectation that I'd be able to complete even the first challenge on my own. It was a good thing Alex and Diego had been available. With Will dead, I would never have had a chance without them.

"I guess it makes sense that Claudia planned for Will to help me, but the whole thing still feels wrong somehow. Are you sure she didn't have someone else finish Will off after you left?"

Zak nodded. "Claudia was as surprised as anyone when you called early. She'd estimated Will wouldn't even be awake at the time the call was received. Of course, she didn't know he'd been shot and that the gunshot had alerted the authorities ahead of schedule. I'm certain her plan was for Will to awaken on his own, find the note and the phone, and either call you or Salinger. When the call came early she looked into it and found out Will had been shot."

I let out a long sigh. "So what now?"

Zak looked at me with an uncertain expression on his face. "I want to find out who did this to Will, but I don't want to put you in danger of any kind. I know you cared about Will and want to find his killer, but you have Catherine to think about."

"I know. And I don't want to put me in danger either, but I do want to help. If Levi and Ellie can stay at the house to help out for a few more days maybe the three of us can put our heads together and ensure that Will's killer is brought to justice."

Zak didn't respond. Salinger didn't either.

"Look, I promise not to go off sleuthing on my own," I said. "The three of us can work together as a team and if there are any dicey interviews to conduct Salinger can handle them."

Still, neither man responded.

I continued. "I need to do this. For Will, who was cheated out of his life. For Phyllis, who was beyond devastated that Will was gone but remained strong enough to help me when we were trying to rescue you. For the kids we're raising, who'll never be safe as long as there are wackos out there who'll shoot a man in the head while he's passed out cold."

I waited for someone to speak. Eventually, Zak did. "Okay. We'll help Salinger, but you have to promise that you won't go off on your own at any time or for any reason."

"I promise."

"Even if all you intend to do is interview a friend you consider to be zero threat."

"I get it. I won't leave the house without one of you with me. I know what's at stake. When I thought you might die it brought home to me how much I want Catherine to grow up with the love and support of both her parents."

Zak took my hand in his and gave it a squeeze. He turned and looked at Salinger. "Were you able to get any physical evidence at all off or around Will's body?"

"Nothing helpful. We know he was shot at close range with a small-caliber handgun. We found one long blond hair on the floor near the body, but it could belong to the maid for all we know. Or maybe Will had a girlfriend. I was so busy trying to figure out where you were, I didn't have a chance to focus on Will's death. Besides, I've figured all along if we found your kidnapper we'd find Will's killer as well. It never occurred to me that the two things were unrelated. I'm still having a hard time wrapping my head around that idea."

"We need a suspect list," I said decisively. "A place to start. And we should bring Phyllis and Ethan in on our brainstorming session. They both worked with him, in addition to being his friends. They may have some ideas of who might want him dead."

"Okay." Salinger stood up. "Why don't you gather together whoever you think should be involved and set up a meeting for this afternoon? I'm heading to Bryton Lake to have a chat with the medical examiner. Maybe he knows, or at least suspects, something he didn't include in his report. Text me a time for the meeting and I'll come over. I should be back in Ashton Falls by one o'clock."

Zak walked Salinger out while I went to find the kids. Based on the voices coming from down the hallway, it sounded like at least some of the current residents of the house were in the den.

******

Zak and I decided to keep the kids home from school for one more day, even though it seemed the threat to them had passed. Levi and Zak had likewise taken the day off from work. Levi, Zak, Alex, and Scooter were holed up in the game room to try out a new game Zak's company had developed, while Ellie and I took Eli, Catherine, and the dogs for a walk.

It was an unseasonably warm day, which served as a reminder that spring was just around the corner. Before long the snow would melt, giving way to the wildflowers that blanketed the area every year. The sky was a pale blue today, contrasting nicely with the dark blue of the lake. I found myself longing for the long, lazy days of summer. It had been a stressful winter and I was ready for the changing of the seasons.

"This warm weather is putting me in the mood to BBQ," I said as we walked along the beach with our babies in backpacks and the dogs running just ahead of us. There were years when we still had six feet of snow on the ground in late March, so the urge to take advantage of the excellent weather was strong.

"I wouldn't mind grilling something for dinner," Ellie replied. "Zak has all those deck heaters we can light if it starts to cool off. I think some fresh air after the past few days will be good for all of us."

"It would be fun to pretend summer has arrived early," I agreed.

"Should we have chicken or steak?"

"Either is fine. We'll go to the store when we get back."

Ellie picked up a stick and threw it for the dogs. Charlie preferred to walk next to me and Zak's dog Bella lumbered along at a slower pace, but Shep, Karloff, and Digger all took off after it, as if beating the others to it was the most important thing in their lives.

"I really appreciate you and Levi putting your lives on hold to help Zak and me with this crazy situation," I said after Karloff returned with the stick and Ellie threw it again.

She took my hand in hers and gave it a squeeze. "You know we're always here for you. No matter what. We're family."

I smiled. "You have no idea how much that means to me. The past two days have been almost unbearable, but it helped a lot that I knew I didn't have to worry about Catherine on top of everything else."

"I just can't believe this isn't over." Ellie sighed as Shep ran up to her with the stick in his mouth. "My heart hurts for Will and everyone who knew and loved him," she said as she tossed it again.

"Yeah." I frowned. "Even though I have no reason to doubt Zak when he insists Claudia didn't kill Will, I'm still having a hard time accepting someone else—possibly someone who knew him—put a bullet in his head." I stopped walking and looked out over the glassy lake. I was physically and emotionally exhausted, but I knew I needed to see the investigation into Will's murder to the end. He'd been a good friend and an excellent employee. He didn't have any family I knew of, but then again, we'd never discussed his family situation except that his wife had died several years ago and his father had passed away shortly after that. He'd never mentioned a mother or siblings to me, which led me to believe he didn't have any. I guess Salinger would sort all that out.

"This weather is putting me in the mood to plant my annual flowers," Ellie said, effectively changing the subject. "Of course, I know frost is inevitable at any time for another two months, so I suppose I'll wait. I meant to put in some bulbs for early color, but I never got around to it."

I knew Ellie was babbling about flowers to distract me from my thoughts about Will, but it wasn't working. Still, there wasn't a thing I could do to help him or to find his killer at the moment, so I smiled at appropriate intervals and asked a few relevant questions when she paused.

When we got back to the house Zak and Levi had lunch on the table. Zak had called Ethan and Phyllis and both would be attending the meeting with Salinger, who thought it might be worthwhile to speak to Brady, because he was also part of the mathematics department at the Academy. Scooter wasn't interested, but Alex wanted to listen in, and after everything she'd done to help me save Zak, I was inclined to let her.

After lunch I took Catherine upstairs to feed her and get her down for a nap. Holding her in my arms as I rocked her while she suckled her bottle was quite possibly one of my favorite things to do these days. I loved the way her little hand cupped the bottle even though she wasn't yet able to hold it on her own. I also loved the way her blue eyes looked directly into mine as she slowly sucked the warm formula from the bottle the two of us held.

After she had finished her bottle I changed her and put her down for her nap. When I got back downstairs Salinger had just arrived and Phyllis, Ethan, and Brady were just pulling into the drive. We all gathered around the dining table and Salinger began the discussion.

"Our purpose today is to try to come up with a list of possible suspects in Will's murder. Any thoughts or observations are of value. If someone has a motive for wanting Will out of the way their name should be brought up even if your feeling is that the individual being discussed doesn't seem the sort to shoot an unconscious man."

Everyone murmured their understanding.

"Ellie has volunteered to take notes. By the time we're finished we hopefully will have a starting point to launch the investigation," Salinger added. "Who'd like to start?"

At first no one spoke. Everyone looked at everyone else. It was apparent there was strong emotion in the room. This conversation wouldn't be easy for any of us.

"I'll start," Phyllis volunteered after a few minutes.

"Okay, go ahead," Salinger urged.

Phyllis shifted nervously in her seat. "Will told me maybe a month ago that he'd begun dating a woman named Alyssa Colter." Phyllis cleared her voice before she continued. Of all of us, I knew this would be hardest on her. "Will met her at a lecture in Bryton Lake. When they realized they both lived in Ashton Falls they decided to have lunch, which led to dinner, which led to weekly dates. At some point they established a physical relationship." Phyllis paused and wiped a tear from the corner of her eye. We all waited in silence, giving her the time she needed before continuing. "A week ago he said he'd decided to break things off with her. He told me that he had only been looking for something casual, but it was becoming apparent Alyssa was interested in something more. The relationship also had become complicated due to the presence of an ex. He didn't say who that was. I suppose you can ask her who she dated before Will. Anyway, the day after we spoke Will came to work with a large scratch on his cheek. I asked him about it and he said he'd talked to Alyssa the night before about taking a step back and she hadn't taken it well. He implied it was a complicated situation with several aspects he didn't want to discuss." Phyllis paused again and looked around at us. "If you're wondering if I think this woman killed Will, not necessarily. I've never met her and have no idea if she has it in her to kill someone. But you did say to bring up the name of anyone who might have a motive to want to hurt Will, and Alyssa sounded pretty upset that he wanted to break up with her."

"Okay. I'll have a chat with her," Salinger said. "Do you happen to know where she lives?"

"Actually, I do," Phyllis answered. "Will mentioned she lived in the condos on River Street. I don't know which unit, but I imagine the property manager can tell you."

"Thank you, Phyllis. That's a good lead." Salinger looked around the table. "Anyone else?"

Alex raised her hand.

"Alex?" Salinger asked.

"I might know something, although I'm pretty sure it's nothing."

Salinger gave her a gentle smile. "We're just gathering information and anything can be helpful. Once we get a list we can start to weed people out."

Alex glanced at me. I nodded.

"Well, I saw Mr. Danner arguing with a student last week. I was called into the office during class to help fill in the blanks on some paperwork my parents had turned in but hadn't completed. I was on my way between the computer lab and the office when I heard shouting. I made a slight detour toward the math wing to check out what was going on. When I turned the corner I found Mr. Danner and Cleveland Brown arguing. They sounded pretty mad."

"Do you know what they were arguing about?" Salinger asked.

"Not really, although it sounded like Cleveland thought Mr. Danner had been treating him unfairly. He said something about his grades affecting his future and some random teacher at a Podunk school wasn't going to derail everything he'd worked for. Mr. Danner said he treated all his students the same, which seemed to make Cleveland even madder. I didn't want to snoop, so I turned around and went on my way."

"Cleveland was carrying a D in Will's class," Zak said. "Cleveland felt the grade was unfair because he'd turned in all his assignments and had done well on the midterm. Will felt that because the class was a practicum, which required participation in class activities and discussions, the grade was fair. He made it clear on the first day of class that most of the students' grade will come from their active participation, not from assignments completed outside of class. Will told me that Cleveland rarely showed up to class and when he did he usually blew off whatever they were doing. It was his opinion that Cleveland felt he didn't have to participate because he was already smarter than everyone else, including the teacher."

Phyllis joined in. "Cleveland has a brilliant mind, but he has an ego and attitude to go with it. I spoke to him about the D, and to Will as well. It seemed to me that Will made it perfectly clear what was expected of students in the class and how it would be graded. He didn't waver from that for any of the other students; everyone was evaluated using the same standards. Apparently, Cleveland felt he should be an exception to the rule; Will disagreed. Cleveland has threatened to get his parents involved, but they're out of the country and can't be reached until sometime next month."

Salinger looked at Ellie. "Add Mr. Brown to the list." He glanced around the room. "Anyone else?"

At first no one spoke. It felt odd to verbalize the observations we made every day that most likely would turn out to be nothing but could, in the end, change a person's life forever, with Salinger in the room. I was aware of the sounds we made as we moved around. The cooling system in the computer room clicked on, seeming abrupt in the otherwise silent room.

"I might know something as well," Brady spoke up after a minute. He swiped at his hair, which had grown long and partially covered one of his eyes. Brady was one of the younger instructors at the Academy. He was a widower with three young children to raise and I appreciated him taking the time to attend the meeting. "But first I want to say I too have had problems with Cleveland Brown, and it wouldn't surprise me a bit if his anger turned to violence. Having said that, I have no actual reason to suspect him of any wrongdoing, though I think it would be worth finding out where he was on Sunday."

The others murmured their agreement.

Brady continued, "Will and I had lunch on Friday of last week. He told me that he was supposed to meet with an old colleague the following day and seemed nervous about it. I asked if he wanted to talk about it, but he was pretty vague. What he did say was that early in his career he worked on a project with another mathematician. He didn't say what the project entailed or who the other mathematician was, but he did share that although they both contributed to the project, for some reason he ended up getting all the credit. Apparently, that led to the relationship with this individual being damaged beyond repair, and he hadn't seen the man in more than two decades. It seems the guy called him out of the blue and wanted to meet. Will didn't want to turn him down, but he was concerned about the reason for the call. I don't know how helpful this is because I don't know who the man was, the location of the meeting, or the name of the project they worked on. Given what happened, I thought it might be important."

Salinger looked around the room. "Did Will mention this to anyone else in the room?"

There was no positive response.

"I can do some snooping," Zak offered. "I might be able to find a paper trail of some sort. If Will was involved in a project for a university or if it was a private contract, there might have been an article written about his findings."

"That sounds like a plan," Salinger said. "Anyone else have anything to add?"

The room feel into silence once again. No one spoke, but from the look of contemplation on the faces around me, I suspected we were continuing to access our memory banks. Everyone wanted to help, but no one wanted to bring up anyone's name out of turn. Simply suggesting someone could have had a beef with Will was likely to make them a suspect.

"Did you locate his next of kin?" I asked Salinger. "A lot of times crimes of passion are carried out by relatives."

Salinger nodded, then dipped his head to consult his notes. His gray hair was beginning to thin a bit on the top, an irrelevant observation, but it struck me as odd that I'd never really noticed it before. I guess he usually wore his hat.

"Danner had no siblings and both of his parents are dead," Salinger began. "The closest relation I found isn't a blood relative but an in-law. It seems his wife had a brother. Danner and the brother-in-law, Evan Strong, seemed to have been close and shared a strong friendship at one time, but after his wife got sick the two disagreed on how to handle her treatment. It seems that drove a wedge between them. After the wife died the two came to blows. I have no reason to believe Strong came to Ashton Falls and shot the man he believed was responsible for his sister's death, but I did find it interesting that when I called him to ask about any relatives he might be aware of, he informed me that he happened to be in town and would bring a list of Danner's distant kin to my office."

I frowned. "He was here? In Ashton Falls? Why?"

"He said he was here to ski," Salinger answered. "And I have no proof that skiing isn't exactly why he came. However, I did find the timing suspect and plan to look in to it further."

After Zak agreed to do the computer thing and obtain phone and banking records as well as all the background info he could find on the four people on our list, Salinger left to begin setting up interviews. I found myself left with nothing to do, which felt unnatural, but I'd promised both Zak and Salinger I'd help where I could while remaining investigation adjacent, so staying out of the fray was exactly what I'd do.

Ethan, Brady, and Phyllis all left as well, and Ellie and I decided to run to the store to get what we'd need to BBQ. We'd chosen a carb-heavy meal of chicken, homemade potato salad, and spicy baked beans, tossed in a salad to add some green, and I suggested strawberry shortcake for dessert, strawberries being a fruit making it a healthy option. I'd been fortunate that I hadn't gained a lot of weight while pregnant with Catherine and after she was born I'd quickly lost what I'd gained, but I still wanted to pay more attention to my diet. I tended to eat a lot of junk and I couldn't help but feel that my terrible diet was the reason I hadn't been able to nurse Catherine for more than a couple of weeks before it became apparent she needed nutrients she wasn't getting from the mama smorgasbord.

"Oh look, they have corn on the cob," Ellie said as we walked down the produce aisle. It was nice to see the spring fruits and veggies beginning to become available. "I haven't had corn on the cob since last summer. Should we get some to grill?"

Personally, I thought potato salad, corn, *and* beans was a bit much, but it did sound good and I'd missed quite a few meals over the past few days. I could certainly afford the extra calories.

"Yeah, let's get some. We'll grill some asparagus as well. I can't wait for watermelon to come in to season. All this summer food is definitely putting me into the mood."

"Oh and peaches." Ellie sighed with a look of longing on her face. "Really juicy ones that drip down your chin when you take a bite."

Yup, it was official: The nice weather had given us both a case of spring fever.

"Is that Zoe Donovan and Ellie Davis?" I heard a loud screech from behind where Ellie and I were picking out ears of corn.

I turned around. "Della Stone?"

"It's me," the plump, cheerful woman standing behind the apples squealed.

"I thought you moved to Kansas."

"I did." Della confirmed as she made her way around the apple bin, trapping me between the bin with the corn and the one with the broccoli. "I followed Donny Baxter to Kansas when he went to work for his uncle's tractor business, but it turned out Donny was a lot more interested in tractors than he was in settling down and starting a family, so I headed to Connecticut, where my cousin lives. I met a guy there who owned his own yogurt shop, and I really thought he would turn out to be my one and only true love, but as it turned out, he'd already given his heart to the Gummy Bear distributer, so I left for Florida, where the men are a bit more mature."

I suddenly remembered why I'd avoided Della in high school. Her tendency to ramble had been legendary. I looked around for Ellie, but she'd managed to make her way down the aisle, leaving me trapped with the overly cheerful woman.

"In Florida I met a man who seemed just perfect for me." Della's monologue slowed a bit and her face grew contemplative. A flash of anger crossed her face, but then she smiled and continued. "He was nice-looking, intelligent, and a lot more mature than any of the guys I'd dated before. He was perfect, but then damn if he didn't up and move away right when I thought he would propose. Anyway, long story short, I made the rounds, but after all was said and done, I ended up right here where I started."

"Welcome back," I said politely, all the while trying to figure out how to extract myself from the conversation without offending Della. In high school she'd been the moody sort. Downright bipolar. And she had a mean streak too. Of course, that was years ago and she was an adult now. I assumed she'd learned to level out her emotions a bit. "Are you planning to stay in the area?"

Della paused and then said, "I'm really not sure. Things haven't gone exactly as I hoped, but it's a new day, so who knows? Things have a way of making themselves right." Della's smile expanded and her eyes grew soft. "I heard you and Ellie both got married and had babies."

"We did get married and have babies," I confirmed. "Ellie married Levi Denton and has a son,

Eli, and I married Zak Zimmerman and we have a daughter, Catherine."

Della raised a brow. "You married Zak Zimmerman? I thought you *loathed* him." Della drew out the word as she said it. "In fact, I can specifically remember you saying he was the most annoying person you'd ever met."

I shrugged. "What can I say? He grew on me."

Della laughed with delight. "Oh, that is just precious. I can't believe how the years have flown by. It seems like yesterday we were drinking sweet wine and skinny-dipping in Miller's Pond."

Skinny-dipping in Miller's Pond was a subject I'd just as soon not discuss in the produce aisle of the market, so I changed the subject. "How's your sister Janet? Is she married? Does she have children?"

"She is married and she has two children." Della's smile faded and her eyes grew hard. I guess after what Della had said about her struggle to find true love that hadn't been the smartest question to ask. "Not to change the subject," she continued, her smile returning as if she didn't have a care in the world, "I ran into one of the women who goes to the same gym I do, and she told me that her sister has a friend who has a friend who told her Will Danner is dead. Is that true? Have you heard?"

I nodded. "It's true. Did you know Will?"

Della shook her head. "Not well. He dated Ali Colter for a while. You remember Ali?"

I frowned. "Actually, I don't. Did she go to our school?"

Della's blond hair fell over her shoulder as she shook her head from side to side. "No, but I introduced her to you at the zombie run six years ago, when I was in Ashton Falls for homecoming."

I tried to remember Della being home six years ago. I had been at the zombie run, but I'd been the one to organize it, so I imagine I'd been busy and hadn't stopped to chat.

"Here." Della opened her purse and took out her phone. She thumbed through her photos until she found the one she was looking for and then handed the phone to me. It was a photo of me standing next to Della. Standing on the other side of her was a tall woman with long blond hair.

"I do kind of remember this. I was working the run that day, so I was pretty busy, and we didn't really talk, but you wanted a photo, so I paused to take one with you. I'm afraid everything happened so fast, I barely remembered the incident, and I certainly didn't recall the name of the woman you were with."

"Her name is Alyssa. Ali is a nickname."

My gaze narrowed. Alyssa was the name of the woman Will had dated recently. I decided to play dumb to see what I could find out. "You said Will and Alyssa dated?"

"Yes. Poor Alyssa. She was so in to him, but I guess he wasn't looking for anything serious. When he broke it off with her she was devastated. When I heard he'd been murdered I thought for a moment she might have done what she kept threatening to do when we spoke on Saturday night. But when I found out he died on Sunday night, I knew she couldn't have."

"And why was that?"

"Because she was with me, getting totally wasted. Men! Right?" Della's face grew hard again. Her blue eyes seemed to grow red with anger. It was obvious some man—or perhaps a bunch of men—had done her wrong. And then just like that, her smile returned and her expression lightened. She chuckled. "That dang Y chromosome does tend to create a package so contrary that hard as you try, you can't live with them, but dang if it doesn't suck to live without them."

"I hear ya!" I said, although I didn't necessarily agree. It just seemed appropriate to show empathy for the heartache she'd obviously suffered. "Can you think of anyone else who might have been mad enough at Will to kill him?"

Ellie hadn't joined the conversation, but she'd maneuvered herself closer to where Della and I were chatting. Out of the corner of my eye, I noticed she was frowning at me. I know she thought I was breaking my promise to Zak not to go off sleuthing on my own, but I wasn't. Not really. I just happened to have run into an old friend at the market and we'd struck up a friendly conversation. Was it my fault she'd brought up the subject of Will's death?

Della tilted her head and lifted a shoulder. "Will seemed like a nice guy, but it was obvious he'd suffered some great pain in his life that prevented him from committing to a relationship. If you ask me, I don't think Alyssa was the first woman to fall in love with him only to find out he was emotionally unavailable." I noticed Della's eyes had grown dark again. "So how did the idiot die anyway?"

"He was shot."

"Seems about right." Della's eyes softened a bit. "It seems to me that he had a long history of ripping the still-beating heart out of whichever woman was foolish enough to fall in love with him."

"I guess it might seem that way." It was true Will enjoyed dating, but it also seemed he was still in love with his dead wife and therefore not emotionally available. I could see how he could completely devastate a young woman. It seemed as if Alyssa had an alibi, though, which meant someone else had shot him. "I know you said you didn't know Will well, but if you're friends with Alyssa, she must have spoken to you about him. Did she ever mention anyone with a specific beef against him?"

Della tapped her chin with her index finger. "I heard Clarissa Holton dated him for a while. I guess you can talk to her. She wasn't as strung out on him as Alyssa, so I have no reason to believe she'd kill him, but she does have a temper. I heard she got into a bar fight with the guy she used to date in high school a while back."

I remembered that too now that Della brought it up. She'd hit the guy over the head with an empty beer bottle when he showed up at her birthday party with the girl who'd been her rival all through school.

"Anyway, like I said, I sort of doubt she was the one to take out her aggravation on the guy, but I suppose it wouldn't hurt to chat her up a bit." Della looked at the phone she still held in her hand. "Look at the time. I really need to git. We should do lunch sometime."

"That would be nice," I said, although I sincerely doubted I would call her.

After we left the grocery store I headed off Ellie's anticipated reprimand for sleuthing with an explanation. "I wasn't sleuthing. I didn't break my promise to Zak. You saw what happened. She came up to me. It would have been rude not to speak to her."

Ellie rolled her eyes.

"Though I do want to call Salinger and tell him about Clarissa, and that Alyssa has an alibi, if you don't mind driving."

"I don't mind a bit. But be sure to tell him that you ran into Della at the store. Ever since he found out you were pregnant he's become almost as protective of you as Zak."

I turned and looked at Ellie. "Did you ever in a million years think Salinger and I would end up being friends? When we first met, he arrested Levi, and then he got me fired from my job. And now we're buddies, through thick and thin."

"The two of you have had an interesting relationship," Ellie agreed.

I smiled as my heart filled with gratitude for the partnership we'd built over time. Salinger had bailed me out of impossible situations, and I knew I'd helped him as well. I guess our friendship was proof that occasionally, oil and water mixed just fine.

Chapter 7

I felt a sense of contentment float across my consciousness as the sky darkened and the moon rose over the distant mountain. The sunset had been a brilliant display of reds and oranges that reflected off the surface of the lake, creating the illusion that the sky and water were burning in a brilliant display of heat and energy. I loved my life at the lake, where the seasons flowed one into the next, each different, but each as spectacular as the others. Initially, when the idea of a BBQ had come to me I'd planned to cook outdoors but eat inside, but it had been such a mild day that Zak had pulled out the heaters. Not only did we BBQ on the deck overlooking the water but we dined outside as well.

I'd suggested to Alex that we might want to invite Diego to dinner as a thank you for all he'd done to save Zak's life. Surprisingly, she'd agreed. We decided to invite Scooter's best friend, Tucker, as well, and as soon as dinner was over all four kids headed to the pool, which my mother's father had designed when he'd built the house and had an indoor/outdoor feature. The ceiling, as well as the walls around the pool, were glass, providing warmth in the winter while maintaining an outdoor feel. During the summer the walls retracted into the exterior walls of the house, creating an outdoor area with easy access to the indoor bath and shower.

I glanced at the kids as they splashed in the water on the other side of the glass. Diego and Alex seemed to be getting along a lot better than they had in the past. I was happy to see that because I really liked him, but I couldn't help but notice that Zak seemed a bit less thrilled with the awakening friendship. In fact, he was glaring at them as they jumped off the diving board together with such a look of fervor that I was afraid he'd bolt out of his lawn chair, march into the house, and demand that they stop having so much fun together.

"Before you go all papa bear with Diego, you might want to consider that he may very well be the reason you're sitting here enjoying this beautiful evening with your family and friends."

Zak's scowl deepened. "Claudia wasn't going to kill me."

"Maybe she would have and maybe she wouldn't. I guess we may never know what would have happened if I'd failed to complete the tasks she gave me. What I do know is that we'd never have gotten through all the tests without Diego's help, and I'm grateful to him for it."

Zak didn't say anything.

"Diego's a good kid. He's smart and confident and, quite frankly, he reminds me a lot of you."

Zak turned and looked at me. "He does?"

I placed my hand on Zak's. "He absolutely does. He's not only brilliant but he's arrogant and cocky, which I think are the traits that initially caused Alex to dislike him. But he's proven to me, and I imagine to Alex too, that he's not only cool and calm in a crisis but he has a good heart and cares about others enough to put himself on the line for them. He didn't have to put his life on hold and help us with Claudia, but he did. And he did it with courage and grace despite the fact that it was very intense at times. He proved to me that he's on his way to becoming a good man. A man who can retain his composure in a crisis. The sort of man I hope both my daughters end up with."

"So now you're marrying Alex and Diego off?"

I laughed. "Hardly. They're kids. But they're bright and capable kids, and I think they complement each other. Diego's good for Alex. She respects him, even though she really didn't like him before Claudia appeared on the scene. Diego understands how she thinks. He knows how to keep her centered when things get tough."

Zak looked back toward the group in the pool. "He does have an exceptional mind. I'd have to say he has more potential than anyone else at the Academy, except Alex, of course."

"So you'll back off and not get in the middle of their friendship?"

He furrowed his brow as he continued to study the kids in the pool. I could see he was struggling with his need to protect Alex from anyone with a Y chromosome who might even glance in her direction. But I knew he wanted what was best for her. "I'll back off for now, but I'll be watching them."

That was probably the best I could hope for. I leaned over and kissed Zak on the cheek, then turned my attention to Ellie and Levi. "So, about Sunday. Are you still up for a party with the kids?"

"We are," Ellie answered. "I can't wait for Eli's first Easter. Will your parents be back?"

I nodded. "They'll be home on Friday. I invited them and Harper, and Jeremy, Jessica, and their two children." Jeremy Fisher was the manager at Zoe's Zoo, the wild and domestic animal rescue and rehabilitation shelter I owned. "Hazel and Grandpa too. They're both anxious to spend time with Catherine on her first Easter. And after all the help they were in the past few days, I think I'll invite Phyllis and Ethan as well."

"I checked the weather forecast and it's supposed to be warm and sunny," Ellie informed me. "We should do the egg hunt on the patio. It'll be cold early in the day, but unless things change it's forecasted to be downright balmy by early afternoon."

"That sounds like fun," I agreed. "Catherine is much too young to care about Easter eggs, but I think she'll get a kick out of having so many kids here. She already loves to watch Eli toddling around. I'm not sure she understands that he's a baby like her and not just one of the dogs, but I've noticed her watching him when he's in the room."

"He *is* the cutest eleven-month-old in town." Ellie chuckled.

I turned back toward Zak. "What do you think? Should we plan an outdoor Easter celebration?"

"If it's warm it should be fine as long as the wind doesn't come up. I'll pull out some additional lawn furniture. I considered doing that anyway. Unless there's a storm lurking in the shadows I think we're in for an early summer this year."

"That'd be okay with me," I replied. "I've been dying to spend some time on the lake. I pretty much missed ski season this year between being pregnant and the lack of snow. If I can't snow ski I may as well waterski."

"I'll see about getting the boat out of storage early this year." Zak looked at his watch. "I told Salinger I'd call him at eight. I'll be in my office if you need me."

"Did you find anything?" I asked. Zak had spent most of the afternoon on the computer pulling phone and banking records for Will as well as doing background searches on each of our suspects.

"Maybe. It's early to know for sure, but I did stumble across a few things Salinger will be interested in." Zak stood up. "Do I need to give Diego a ride home? This could take a while."

"I'll give him a ride," Levi volunteered.

After Zak went into the house Ellie and I did the dishes while Levi and Eli joined the kids in the pool. Eli was too young to swim, but he loved floating around in his little toddler tube. Levi kept one hand on the tube just in case, while Eli laughed and kicked his feet in the warm water. I supposed Catherine would be old enough for her own tube in the summer. As a new mother, I couldn't wait to experience all the firsts in her life, although in a way I wanted time to slow down so I could really enjoy each stage of her development. I glanced at Alex and Scooter and thought about how much they'd changed since they'd come to live with us. I adored the teenagers they'd become, but at times I missed the sweetness of the children they'd been. Life was a journey that ensured that each moment wasn't stagnant, things constantly changing. I supposed that was a good thing even when they changed a bit too fast for my taste.

******

Later that evening, Zak and I cuddled on our bed with Catherine laying between us. We were both on our sides with our heads resting on our hands, while our elbows rested on the mattress. Catherine kicked her legs and smiled as she cooed about something she probably believed we understood. I loved this time of the day, between dinner and bedtime. Most often it was spent enjoying the fascinating new human who had come into our lives. I'd missed our daughter and our bedtime ritual while I'd been rushing around trying to save her daddy, so the fact that she seemed extra-alert and wanted to play was fine with me.

Charlie was on the bed between Zak and me just below where Catherine was resting. He watched her with what looked to be a smile on his face. I loved my friends and my extended family, but I found I most cherished these moments when it was just the four of us. Zak put a finger near Catherine's hand. She grabbed it and let out a little scream of delight.

"I think she's happy to have you home," I said as I chuckled at her antics.

"And I'm happy to be here." Zak continued to let Catherine hold his finger, but he turned his gaze to me. "I'm so sorry you had to go through all that. I can't imagine how truly horrific it must have been."

"It wasn't my favorite time, that's for sure." A single tear slid down my cheek. "With each new test I was presented I had no idea if I would find a way to solve it or if I'd fail and you'd die."

Zak leaned forward and kissed the tear from my cheek. He paused and looked deeply into my eyes while Catherine lay tented between us. "I knew from the moment Claudia explained her sick game to me that she was going to send you to hell and back. I felt so helpless and I knew that no matter how badly I wanted to help you there was absolutely nothing I could do." Zak leaned back and put some distance between us.

"Did she ever explain why she did it?" I asked.

"No. As I said, when she first kidnapped me I thought she wanted something from me, but when she told me her actual plan, I felt like I'd been kicked in the stomach. I wasn't worried about me, but I knew that if you failed and I died you would never be able to live with yourself, and that was something I just couldn't live with."

"The tests were hard. Some of them were *really* hard, but luckily, we have smart, talented friends who helped me." I stroked Catherine's head with my finger. "Why do you think she went to the lengths she did? If her file from the NSA was really what she was after why didn't she just kidnap you and force you to steal it for her? It must have taken her hours to set up all the challenges she provided to me."

"I don't know for certain, but I think she enjoyed playing with you. Playing with us. She reminded me of a cat with a mouse she keeps batting around rather than having some mercy on the poor thing and killing it. I was alone much of the time, but there were a few occasions when she came into the room where she was holding me and it seemed like she was having the best time. She actually chuckled."

I twisted my lips. "I'm glad someone was having fun. I never want to have the life of someone I love riding on my ability to keep up with a woman who's clearly a genius again."

I laughed as Catherine let out a squeal of delight when she realized Charlie had scooted around close enough for her to grab a fistful of his fur. I winced when she gave it a good hard tug, but Charlie looked like he was in heaven just being touched by his little sidekick. "Do you think the feds have caught up with Claudia?" I asked as Catherine began kicking her legs even harder than before.

"Not that I've heard. She's probably long gone. She let herself get caught once. My feeling is she'll be a lot more careful now that she's finally free."

"Do you think our paths will cross again?"

Zak's face grew contemplative. I knew he'd been asking himself that same question. "I hope not, but I suppose it's a possibility. We need to learn to be aware of everyone around us. If Claudia wants to make her way back into our lives for some reason it'll be hard to avoid her. She can really look like anyone."

I thought about the old woman in the bar who'd handed me the envelope and wondered if that had been Claudia. Could she have been in the pool hall when I'd gone there to look for the first set of clues? With her talent as a master of disguise she could have been anywhere and everywhere and I would never have known. As much as I feared Claudia, I was determined not to let her get into my head. It would be too easy to let someone like her turn me into a paranoid individual.

I ran a finger down Catherine's arm. She looked to be getting sleepy. I wanted to ask Zak about his research that day and what he'd found, but we'd agreed to put the investigation into Will's death on the back burner until tomorrow. Salinger was coming for coffee in the morning, so I'd have my answers soon enough. Catherine let out a yawn followed by a hiccup. I could tell she was ready for bed, so I sat up and lifted her into my arms. I carried her into the nursery and gently placed her in the crib. I leaned forward and kissed her dark head before rejoining Zak in the bedroom.

"I guess I'm pretty tired too," I said as I laid down on the bed next to him.

"I'm ready to turn in," Zak agreed. "I just need a minute to wash up."

I removed the extra pillows from the bed and pulled back the comforter. I made sure the fireplace was clicked off and that all the windows were closed and locked. Normally, I'd check on Alex and Scooter, but they were both watching a movie with Levi. Zak came out of the bathroom wearing only a pair of boxers. He'd taken a quick shower and his hair, still damp, curled slightly behind his ears. As tired as I was, I felt my stomach tighten at the sight of his bare chest, hard and defined. Although Zak and I had been together for a number of years, I was as attracted to him now as I'd been the first time he'd come into my bedroom with a bare chest and passion in his eyes.

He turned off the lights and crawled into the bed beside me. He pulled me into his arms, so I rested on my side with my head on his chest, listening to his strong, steady heartbeat. Had it only been yesterday when I'd truly doubted I'd ever hear that heartbeat again?

I ran my hands over Zak's chest as I tried to distract myself from the terror that still lurked at the back of my mind. We'd been through a lot together in the years we'd been a couple, but I wasn't sure I'd ever felt quite so vulnerable as I had these past few days. To know at any moment that one mistake could make that one his last was truly more than I'd had time to process. Zak wasn't only my love. He was my best friend. He was my life. He was the image I saw when I looked in to the future. I didn't know what I'd do if I ever lost him.

Zak's arms tightened around my body as my hand worked itself lower. He pulled me onto his chest and I lowered my lips to his. I began to relax as his kiss deepened, distracting me from my thoughts.

I knew life didn't come with guarantees. But I also knew we were each provided with a sequence of moments that made up our lives, ours to spend as we chose. I could spend my moments dwelling on the fear that had been awakened within me. I could let the fear dominate my life until I was but a shell of the person I'd once been. Or I could quell the fear that nagged at the edge of my mind. The choice was mine and mine alone.

As Zak's hands caressed my skin, I made a choice to focus on the gentle embrace of the man beneath me.

Chapter 8

Wednesday, March 28

I woke once again to an empty bed. I rolled onto my side and looked at the window at the brilliant sunshine. I smiled. After a long night of lovemaking I felt I had a new lease on life. I rolled out of bed and pulled on my robe. I could hear voices downstairs, so I assumed the rest of the household was up before me. I headed into Catherine's room to find her crib empty. It seemed she was spending quality time with Daddy this morning. Taking advantage of the free time, I hopped into the shower. I let the hot water roll over my body as the remainder of the tension I'd been holding seemed to melt away. It had been such a difficult couple of days, but now that it was over I willed myself to think happier thoughts. Thoughts of Catherine's first Easter and the party I'd been planning when Zak was kidnapped. Thoughts of the longer days and warmer weather, which naturally led to thoughts of long, lazy days on the beach with the kids or on the boat with Zak as the sun set on the horizon.

After I'd shampooed and conditioned my hair I dressed in a pair of jeans and a sunny yellow top. I pulled a white hooded sweatshirt over it because the morning temperature still lingered in the thirties, then finger combed my hair and headed downstairs. When I arrived in the kitchen I found Zak sitting at the table talking to Salinger. Was finding him in my kitchen going to become a regular thing?

I leaned over and kissed Zak on the lips. "Where's everyone else?"

"Alex and Scooter went to school and Levi went to work," Zak answered. "Ellie had her mommy-and-me class this morning, so she took Catherine along with her and Eli. She was going to wake you to see if you wanted to go too but I told her to let you sleep."

I felt a momentary pang of disappointment. Ellie had been going to mommy-and-me gatherings since Eli was six months old and had learned to crawl. Catherine wasn't quite old enough to care about the various games the moms played with their babies, but she liked seeing everyone, so we'd started tagging along and watching from the sidelines. Watching the mothers interact with their babies had been good for me as well. As much as I loved Catherine and enjoyed spending time with her, being a mother wasn't something I came by naturally. It helped to see how other mothers dealt with the little challenges that presented themselves throughout the day.

I poured myself a cup of coffee and sat down with the men. Ellie would be home with the babies in less than an hour, so I should make the best use of my time.

"Salinger just caught me up on what he's learned and I was about to fill him in on what I found in my research yesterday," Zak continued.

"Care to provide the condensed version?" I asked.

Salinger cleared his throat. "I spoke to Alyssa Colter, who verified that she was with Della Stone all afternoon and into the evening on the day Will was shot. She did say she'd been by Will's motel room to speak to him earlier in the day. She hoped she could say something to make him reconsider his stance on their relationship, but he wasn't interested. She also admitted to being angry enough to shoot him, but she insists she didn't. I spoke to Della's neighbor, who said there was a lot of noise coming from Della's house that day. She was aware they'd been drinking, so she assumed they both were at Della's home at the time the shooting occurred."

"So I guess we can take her off the list." I took a sip of coffee. "Did you speak to Clarissa Holton?"

"I did," Salinger answered. "She also admitted to having been hurt and angered by Will's commitment issues, but she had an alibi. It seems she worked at the church spaghetti feed on Sunday. I verified that with one of the women who volunteered with her."

"And Cleveland Brown?" I asked, bringing up the student Alex had seen arguing with Will prior to his death.

"Went home for the weekend. His roommate and mother both confirmed that."

"So that leaves the brother-in-law who just happened to be in town and the man who blamed him for stealing the spotlight on the project they worked on together," I said.

"I still haven't been able to come up with the name of the man Brady referred to, but I'm working on it. I did speak to the brother-in-law. Strong claims he's here to ski and that he was on the mountain doing just that on the day Will was shot. Unfortunately, he went skiing alone, so that's difficult to verify. He used his pass several times that day, but his last run was at three twenty-eight. Will died several hours later, so having been on the mountain isn't really an alibi."

"Did you ask about his activities after skiing?"

Salinger gave me a look. "This isn't my first dog-and-pony show."

"Of course. I'm sorry. Go on."

"Strong said he picked up takeout and ate it in his hotel room while watching a movie on television. I've been unable to confirm that because no one seems to have noticed whether he was in his room. I still consider him a suspect, especially because he had nothing but negative things to say about Will and the way he approached the treatment of his sister's illness."

"The thing that doesn't fit with Strong as the killer is that Will's wife died years ago. Why would this man come to Ashton Falls so much later and kill his brother-in-law? If Will's wife had died recently I could maybe buy Strong as the killer, but the time lag doesn't make sense."

Salinger shrugged. "I agree. But coming to Ashton Falls to ski when there are plenty of other places to go doesn't make sense either. It's not like we've had a great year for snow. The ski areas are struggling to cover the runs. If the only thing Strong was after was a weekend on the slopes why didn't he go to Aspen, where the skiing's much better this year?"

"Good point." I took another sip of my coffee. "Anything else?"

"Nothing conclusive." Salinger looked at Zak. "Unless you have something."

"I might," Zak responded. He shifted in his chair so he could lean over to take a file from the top of the stack he'd placed on the table next to him. "First, I looked at Will's financial and phone records. The former didn't suggest anything unusual, but I did notice a check he'd written and then stopped payment on. It was for a large amount, almost forty thousand dollars, so I took a closer look. It seems the check was to pay one of the subcontractors, Trenton Cline, for work done on his home. He'd installed new cabinets in the kitchen. I spoke to Mr. Cline, who'd filed a lawsuit against Will for failure to meet his financial obligation. I looked in to it further and learned Will canceled the check when he found out the cabinets were made of fiberboard covered with hardwood, rather than solid hardwood. According to the statement Will provided to his attorney, he was very clear that he wanted hardwood to be used throughout." Zak paused and then continued. "I spoke to Mr. Cline. He insists Will ordered cabinets made of alder from a catalog and that the cabinets in the photos were made using a wood overlay. I don't know who's wrong and who's right here. I guess the court would have figured that out. What I do know is that Mr. Cline was about as angry as I've ever seen a man. According to him, when Will canceled his check it put his account into the red and a bunch of checks he'd written bounced. He said he's afraid he might lose his business over it."

"That sucks," I said. "And I understand he'd be angry, but what would he gain from killing Will? If the lawsuit had been heard he eventually might have gotten his money, but now who knows if he ever will?"

"I don't disagree with that train of thought," Zak said, "and I would most likely have let the whole thing go, but I looked into Mr. Cline's finances and found that fifty thousand dollars had been debited from his account the day after Will died. The money goes back to a hard money lender, so it's possible Mr. Cline borrowed the money to pay his debts, but the timing bothers me, so I'm looking into it further."

"I'll add him to my suspect list," Salinger said. "Let me know what you find out."

"I will," Zak answered.

Salinger's phone rang and he excused himself to take the call.

"You look well rested," Zak said, tucking a lock of my unruly hair behind my ear.

I smiled. "Very well rested. And a lot more relaxed as well. Are you taking today off?"

"Yes and no. I don't plan to go to the Academy today, but I do plan to spend time working in my home office. I've been trying to figure out the identity of the man Will was talking about when he told Brady he was meeting a man who held a grudge against him for stealing all the glory on a project they'd worked on together. I have a few ideas, but so far I haven't narrowed it down as much as I'd like."

"Speaking of projects, what about the one you and Will were working on? I know it's some sort of top secret deal. Could it have gotten Will killed?"

Zak frowned. "The thought has crossed my mind. Very few people even knew Will and I were working together, so my inclination is to believe his death isn't related to the project, though I suppose I shouldn't eliminate any possibility."

I got up to refill my coffee cup. "If Claudia's purpose for showing up at Will's room was to kidnap you how did she know you were even there? It's not like the meeting was planned. In fact, it seemed sort of sudden."

"I received a text from Will saying we needed to meet. I texted back that I'd come to the motel because you were napping. When I arrived Will jumped right in, telling me he was glad I'd decided to stop by because he had some ideas to run past me. We didn't really compare notes as to who texted whom first until after we'd ordered the pizza. Will made a comment about hijacking the conversation and wondered why I'd wanted to meet in the first place. I said it hadn't been my idea to meet, that I'd only texted him in response to his text to me. He insisted that while he was glad I'd stopped by, he hadn't wanted to invade my family time and had decided to wait to speak to me about his idea until the next day at work. He assured me that he hadn't been the one to send the text. That was when we realized something odd was going on, but it was just about then that Claudia showed up at the door with the pizza and we never did have the chance to figure it all out."

"Have you figured it out now?" I asked.

"Someone—I'm assuming Claudia—cloned Will's phone and sent me the text. I have no idea how she knew Will was at the motel or that we'd been working together and meeting there. I suppose she might have been following me for a while. When she can look like anyone it's pretty much impossible to realize you have a tail."

"Yeah, I get that. She's very good at what she does."

I looked up as Salinger walked back into the room. "I have to go. I'll call you this afternoon to touch base."

"Is everything okay?" I asked. He had a worried look on his face.

"There's a pileup on the highway. It sounds bad. I may be there a while."

******

Zak went into his office and I made myself something to eat. By the time I'd finished my breakfast Ellie had returned with the babies. We decided to feed and change them and then head into town, hoping they'd nap in their strollers while we looked for Easter baskets and stuffed bunnies. It was close to lunchtime, so we decided to eat in town as well. It would be nice to have a day out with my best friend without having to think about death, suspects, and murder motives.

"I found the cutest outfit for Eli to wear on Sunday," Ellie said after we'd settled into a booth at Rosie's Café and ordered seafood salads with ice tea to drink. "Levi isn't a fan of the bunnies on the front. He doesn't think they're masculine enough for his son. But I reminded him that the outfit was blue and white and therefore very masculine, and the little white bunnies were simply a tribute to the holiday. Have you found something special for Catherine?"

"Not yet. I saw a cute outfit at the boutique on Main, but I never had the opportunity to go back by for a second look. It's probably gone by now."

Ellie shrugged. "Maybe it is and maybe it isn't. We'll head over there when we're done here. You know I adore Eli, but it would be fun to have a girl to buy frilly dresses for."

"Actually, the outfit I was looking at was denim overalls with a bunny on the butt."

"Overalls?" Ellie seemed shocked. "Catherine's a girl. You should buy a dress for her first Easter. Something frilly, with a ruffle."

I frowned. "Really? Ruffles? Seems a bit much for a three-month-old. She'll probably puke on whatever I get her by noon anyway. Overalls and a onesie seem a lot more practical. And I did say there was a bunny involved. Seems Eastery to me."

Ellie rolled her eyes but didn't comment. I had a feeling a frilly dress was in Catherine's future whether either of us wanted one or not.

"By the way," Ellie said, changing the subject, "I ran into Nancy Dillard at mommy-and-me today. She said to say hi, by the way." Nancy had worked as a waitress at Rosie's back when Ellie's mother owned the restaurant and Ellie worked there. She'd married and had twin boys and was now a full-time mom. "She was having lunch with a friend on Saturday of last week and ran into Will having lunch with a man she didn't recognize."

"I wasn't aware Nancy knew Will."

"Her parents own the motel where he was living while his house was being worked on. It seemed he liked to sit out on the patio near the pool when the weather was nice, even though the pool was closed for the season. She ran into him a number of times when she was visiting her parents and they'd struck up conversations. You know what a math geek Nancy is. I never did understand why she didn't go to college."

Ellie had a point. Nancy definitely had been overqualified to be a waitress, but she'd seemed to like the work and was a very likable woman, so she'd cleaned up when it came to tips.

"Anyway," Ellie continued, "Nancy described the man Will was with as being tall—at least six feet three or four inches—and very thin. She said he looked like a pencil. He had dark brown hair cut conservatively and he wore glasses, wire-framed. She also said he was overdressed for the venue, wearing a white dress shirt with dark dress slacks. I don't know if that's important information, but I thought you should know."

"Did Nancy say if she spoke to Will?" I asked.

"She said she didn't. She waved at him, but he was so focused on his conversation that he didn't notice, and she didn't want to interrupt. She said both men seemed really intent on what they were discussing. In fact, they both were holding their forks but neither was eating."

"Did Nancy tell this to Salinger?"

"No. She said he interviewed her parents, but he hadn't contacted her. Not that he'd have a reason to, because she wasn't at the motel when the shooting occurred and her parents weren't aware she'd run into

Will, so they wouldn't have brought it up. She thought about calling the sheriff's office, but she admitted Salinger intimidates her. He pulled her over for speeding once and he made it seem like she'd assassinated the president or something. In her words, 'the guy is way too intense.'"

I could see how Salinger could come off that way. I mean, he'd arranged for me to be fired from a job I'd had since I'd been a teenager on our first encounter. "Okay, thanks. I'll mention it to him. He was called out to deal with an accident, but he said he'd check in with us this afternoon. I've been told not to sleuth if Zak or Salinger aren't with me, so I'm not going to, but I'm dying to try to figure out who Will met for lunch. I don't suppose it would put us in any danger to talk to the waitstaff as long as we're here. Someone might know who the tall man with the wire-rimmed glasses was."

"Don't," Ellie said. "I know you. You're like a dog with a bone. A few questions will lead to new questions, and before you know it we'll be heading across town to check out some lead. You'll ask me to wait in the car with the babies and I will. You'll assure me you won't be in any danger, but you always seem to end up in something awful. I'll realize you're in trouble and I'll have to try to decide what to do, help you or stay with the babies as I promised. I'll end up staying with the babies because it'll seem like the right thing to do, knowing all the while that some madman is going to kill you any moment. Eventually, Salinger will arrive, but will it be in time? Who needs the stress?"

I laughed. "You've thought about this, haven't you?"

"Since the moment you told me you were pregnant. Now, let's go buy Catherine a frilly dress and forget about all this sleuthing nonsense."

"Okay," I reluctantly agreed. I'd known being sidelined would be tough; I just hadn't known how tough.

Chapter 9

Salinger stopped by later in the afternoon, after Ellie and I had come home from shopping. Both Eli and Catherine were sitting happily in their swings while Ellie looked on from her spot on the sofa, where she was reading a parenting magazine.

After Zak poured everyone something to drink, he started right in. "I think I may have identified the man Will was talking about when he spoke to Brady." Zak slid a photo of a tall, thin man with wire-rimmed glasses to the center of the table.

"That's the man Ellie told me that Nancy saw having lunch with Will on Saturday," I blurted out.

Both Zak and Salinger looked at me.

"Ellie and I had lunch at Rosie's. That reminded Ellie that she'd spoken to a woman who used to waitress there back when she worked there too. Nancy was at mommy-and-me with Ellie and mentioned to her that she'd seen Will in the café with a man she didn't recognize on the day before he was shot. She said he was tall and thin with dark hair and wire-rimmed glasses." I pointed to the photo. "Tall and thin with wire-rimmed glasses. This has to be the guy."

"Did Ellie say if Nancy happened to catch his name?" Salinger asked.

"No. Nancy said she waved at Will, but he was so focused on the other man he didn't seem to notice her. She didn't want to interrupt them. I bet this guy has been nursing a grudge for however many years and finally flipped out."

Zak frowned. "I kind of doubt it, but I don't suppose it's outside the realm of possibility."

Salinger turned his attention to Zak. "What exactly did you find out?"

"The man in the photo is Wesley Riverton. He graduated college at about the same time as Will and both were offered jobs with Wentworth Industries, based in Central California. Wentworth was a startup company thirty years ago, but they were a company with vision. Their focus was on new technology, strictly innovative, cutting-edge stuff. Apparently, Will and Wesley were assigned to work together on a project that would revolutionize communications the way we know it. They did the math, came up with a concept, and built a prototype, which Wentworth ended up selling to the military. The application of the project was classified, but Wentworth, and Will Danner, were suddenly primetime news. I don't know why Wesley Riverton wasn't part of the media coverage. Wentworth Industries went on to become a global, multibillion-dollar company, Will received job offers that, had he accepted them, would have sent his career onto the fast lane, and Wesley was never heard from again."

"That doesn't seem fair," I said.

"Unless there was something else going on that I don't know about, it wasn't fair," Zak agreed.

"What about Danner?" Salinger asked. "You said he received job offers that would have launched his career if he'd accepted one of them. He didn't accept any?"

Zak shook his head. "After the media circus died down he got married and took a job at a small private university. I have no idea why, although life in the fast lane isn't for everyone, and from what I knew of Will, I doubt it was a lifestyle he was cut out for."

"Okay, so all these years later this Wesley guy shows up in Will's life and wants to meet? Why?" I asked.

Zak shrugged. "I guess with Will dead you'll have to ask Wesley. And by you, I mean Salinger."

"Do we know if he's still in town?" Salinger asked.

"I couldn't find evidence that he is, but I haven't found anything to the contrary either," Zak answered. "I'll keep looking."

I sat back and let everything sink in a bit. I felt like we were getting somewhere, but were we? "Okay, so at this point we have Wesley Riverton, who we're pretty sure had lunch with Will on the day before he died, as a suspect, as well as the brother-in-law, Evan Strong. Anyone else?"

"I managed to get the manager at the hotel where Strong has been staying to give me the contact information of the couple in the room next to his on Sunday night. According to them, the television in

135

Strong's room was on until after midnight," Salinger reported. "That doesn't prove Strong was in the room the entire time, but it does seem to support his story."

"So if Strong was telling the truth, that only leaves Wesley Riverton or the cabinet guy," I summed up.

"I checked further into Trenton Cline's finances," Zak said. "The money that was deposited into his account was a loan. I verified it with the lender. I don't think Cline is our guy. It seems Will's death actually hurt his chances of recovering what he feels he's owed."

"So it has to be Riverton," I said.

"Or someone who hasn't yet come to mind," Salinger countered. "Either way, I'd like to have a chat with him. I'll see what I can find out." Salinger looked at Zak. "Let me know if you manage to track him down first."

After Salinger left Zak and I decided we could use some fresh air, so we bundled up Catherine and put her in the baby pack while I rounded up the household dogs. It was another beautiful sunny day. Ashton Falls had experienced some truly horrific March storms in the past, but it looked like this year it was going to come in and go out like a lamb.

"It feels like May," Zak said as we strolled along the beach. "I keep thinking this weather can't possibly hold, but so far…"

"Don't jinx it," I warned Zak. "I love the snow, but this year I'd prefer to glide into the change of seasons without the drama of early spring storms."

"I agree. I'm ready for some warm weather. I think the kids are beginning to get spring fever as well. Scooter asked me last night when we were going to get the boat out of storage. The way the weather is now, I'm tempted, but I've lived in the area long enough to know a mild March can lead to a cold April."

I leaned my head on Zak's shoulder as we walked, enjoying the time we had in the sunshine, especially if it wasn't destined to last. The five dogs who were rambling along with us were chasing each other into the lake and then back out onto the sand again. They were going to need a good rinsing when we got home.

"Did you get what you need for Easter?" Zak asked.

I nodded. "Ellie talked me into a dress for Catherine that I'm not too sure about, but otherwise I think we're ready. We have a menu, though we still need to buy the food, we have eggs to hide for the older kids, baskets for everyone ten and under, and games and outdoor toys for the older kids."

"Sounds great. I can't remember the last time I looked forward to a holiday the way I am this one."

I squeezed Zak's arm. "I'm just glad we'll *all* be here to celebrate Catherine's first Easter."

Zak turned and kissed me on the top of the head. "Me too. I try not to think about what we went through with Claudia, but it's hard to put it out of my mind completely."

"Have you spoken to Shredder at all?" I asked.

"Yes, I have. He couldn't confirm where Claudia is now, but he did say she'd left the country and he was hot on her trail. I got the impression she was being her slippery self, so capturing her was in no way guaranteed. But I also think he won't give up no matter how long it takes."

"It must be lonely being him," I said. "Always chasing after someone and never really having the chance to settle down and have what we have." I ran a hand over Catherine's dark hair.

"I suppose it's the life he chose."

I frowned. "I'm not sure about that. At least not entirely. I sort of have the feeling he tried to get out and settle in one place when he moved to Hawaii, but something happened and he was pulled back in. He didn't say as much, but when I spoke to him it sounded like he was going to make a move of some sort."

"He's leaving Hawaii?" Zak asked.

"Maybe. You know Shredder; he's not one for sharing, but I picked up a vibe when I spoke to him. Of course, we were trying to save your life, so it's not like we entered into some sort of deep personal conversation. Still, I wouldn't be surprised to find he'd relocated the next time we talk to him. Like Claudia, he seems to be constantly in a state of motion. Hovering from time to time, but never really stopping and putting down roots."

Zak abruptly changed the subject. "Speaking of roots, I think the big tree in the front died over the winter. I was thinking of replacing it with a maple. The fall color will be nice, and maples tend to do well around here."

"A maple would be nice," I agreed, completely aware of how absurd it was to have discussed murder suspects, a top-secret black ops agent and his life choices, and a new tree for the drive within the span of less than fifteen minutes.

I suppose life is what you make of it, and we seemed to be working on a colorful but illogical abstract of some sort.

******

The danger seemed to have passed, so Levi and Ellie decided to head home. We still didn't know who'd killed Will, but, unlike the madwoman who had kidnapped Zak, we didn't feel the killer posed a danger to the family. Zak and Salinger had spoken again on the phone and had decided the prime suspect was Wesley Riverton. Not only had Will stolen his limelight on a project they'd worked on together, but Zak had continued to dig and had found that Riverton had dated the woman who would eventually become Will's wife before he had. As far as Zak could tell, Will hadn't only stolen Riverton's glory but his woman as well.

"I've been craving a big juicy hamburger all day," I said to Zak later that afternoon as we began to discuss dinner preparations.

"We don't have either ground sirloin or fresh rolls, but I'd be happy to run to the market to get some if you'd like. It's nice enough again this evening to grill the meat."

I picked up my keys. "Catherine is napping and the older kids are occupied. Why don't you make a pasta salad to go with the burgers and I'll run to the market? Do we need anything else?"

"Maybe another carton of milk, but otherwise I think we're good for a couple of days."

I kissed Zak on the lips. "Okay. I won't be long. There's a bottle of formula in the refrigerator all ready to go if Catherine wakes up."

Unfortunately, the market was crowded at this time of day; people with nine-to-five jobs were just beginning to get off. I grabbed what I needed and went to the checkout. I found a line with just two people in front of me, so I slipped into it just before at least ten other people got there behind me. Today must be my lucky day; normally, I'd be the one to get into line just *after* ten other people made the decision to do the same thing.

"Zoe, fancy meeting you twice in one week," Della Stone greeted me as I slid into line behind her, not realizing who was just before me.

Drat. I'd really hoped to get out of the market quickly.

"Had a hamburger craving," I said, hoping my brief reply would serve as a hint that a lengthy conversation wasn't desired.

Della held up a box. "Mac and cheese. I don't know what it is about the stuff, but when I'm feeling really down mac and cheese is the only thing that can make the world seem right again."

A really good friend would ask Della why she'd been feeling down, but I just wanted to pay for my items and get home to Zak and the kids, so I smiled and didn't reply. Della only had three items, so she was able to check out quickly. I waved and sighed with relief as she headed toward the exit minus the long conversation I'd been afraid she'd trap me into engaging in.

I paid for my own groceries and headed toward my car. That was when I noticed Della standing in front of her car with the hood up.

Pretend you don't see her, I mentally schooled myself as I walked briskly to my vehicle. I slipped my one bag onto the backseat and had opened the driver's side door when I caught Della out of the corner of my eye.

"Damn," I said out loud as I closed the door. I walked over to where she was standing. "Is there a problem with your car?" I found myself asking almost against my will.

"It won't start," Della said with tears in her eyes. "Talk about a perfectly horrible end to a perfectly horrible day."

"I'm not a mechanic, but I can help you get a tow truck if you'd like," I offered.

"I have ice cream that will melt if I wait for a tow. If you can give me a ride home I'll call a friend to help get the car started."

I wanted to groan, but instead I smiled. "I'd be happy to give you a ride. Grab your bag and we'll get going."

"Thank you so much," Della said. She opened the back door of her car to reveal the presence of ten bags rather than the one I was expecting.

"You have a lot more than I thought," I said as Della picked up the first bag.

"I made a few stops before I came here. I hope you have room in your trunk for all this."

"Yeah." I sighed. "Me too."

I pulled my car around so we could load Della's stuff directly into my trunk. Luckily, the small house she'd rented was only about five minutes from the market. When we arrived I pulled into her driveway and began to help her unload her belongings. A bottle fell out of the first bag and onto the floor of my trunk. I picked it up. "Moonshine?" I asked after reading the logo on the bottle.

"The real stuff, imported from Kentucky. I found a little liquor shop just outside of town that sells it. The stuff is *goooood*," Della said, stringing out the word.

"Is it strong?"

"Oh yeah." Della smiled. "You have to get used to it and know how to sip it real slow. Alyssa and I were sipping on it last Sunday when she was over, but she was so upset over Will that she didn't take it slow like she should have and ended up passing out after only an hour. That girl is a bit of a lightweight."

I slipped the bottle back into the bag. I supposed the fact that Alyssa wasn't only with Della when Will was shot but was passed out provided an even more solid alibi. Once I had a bag in each arm I followed Della to the front door. After she unlocked it I followed her to the kitchen, where I set the two bags on the counter.

I was heading back through the living area to grab the next two bags when I noticed a photo of Will with Della. Odd; hadn't she said they didn't know each other all that well? I paused and took a closer look at the photo. Based on the background, it hadn't been taken in Ashton Falls. It looked like it had been taken in…

"Florida," Della said. "Daytona Beach, to be exact."

I turned and looked at Della, who was standing behind me. "I didn't know you knew Will before he came to Ashton Falls." It was then I noticed the hardness in her eyes.

"Will and I first met in Florida. He was teaching at a small university where I worked part time in the bookstore."

I glanced at the photo again. Suddenly, I realized that when Will had mentioned to Phyllis that an ex had come into the picture, complicating his relationship with Alyssa, it was *his* ex and not *hers*, as I'd assumed. "Will is the man you dated while living in Florida who left and broke your heart?"

Della laughed, although the sound wasn't one of humor or glee. It was more of a laugh of insanity. "Will and I were supposed to get married. I loved him and I thought he loved me. We had such a bright future, but then his old man died and he decided he needed a change. He told me that he cared about me and that he'd always value our time together, but then he told me he'd decided to move back to Ashton Falls. Ashton Falls! The very place where I'd grown up. I mean really, what are the odds?"

I had no idea what the odds were, though I bet Will could have figured them out.

"I was devastated, but of course I couldn't let him know that. I figured once he left he would begin to miss me, so I pretended to be fine with his decision and let him go. You see, my plan was to give him some space and then show up for a visit, acting all surprised when I ran in to him."

"But it didn't work out that way," I realized.

Della's eyes flashed with rage. "No, it didn't. Imagine my surprise when I showed up in town to find he'd not only moved on but moved on with one of my best childhood friends. I was the one he loved.

I was the one he was supposed to be pining over. I was the one he was supposed to devote his life to."

Suddenly, everything was falling into place. I really wished it hadn't. I took a step toward the door. "We should get the rest of your stuff."

"Not so fast." Della crossed the room. She opened a drawer and pulled out a gun.

"You're going to shoot me?"

"I don't want to." I noticed Della's hand was shaking. "But I can tell by the look on your face that you've figured out I was the one who shot Will."

I didn't deny it; I don't have much of a poker face, so I was sure I was revealing my thoughts as they played through my mind. "Why?"

Della began to cry. "I don't know. I didn't mean to hurt him. I was drunk and angry, but I never, ever consciously made the decision to kill him. I don't even remember driving there. It was like I was in some sort of a trance. One minute I was sitting in my living room drinking moonshine and complaining to my best friend, who had long since passed out, that life wasn't fair and I deserved to have a man to love. The next thing I knew, I was standing in Will's motel room with a gun in my hand. When I saw the blood everywhere I panicked. I took off and never told anyone."

I kept my eye on Della's hand. She still held the gun but loosely, and it was pointed at my feet rather than my head.

"I'm sorry, Della. I can't imagine how hard it must have been for you to give your heart to a man who didn't return your love."

Della looked at me through her tears. "I'm a good person. Most people like me. Men even like me, but no man has ever *loved* me. Not the way I loved them. Why is that?"

"I don't know." I supposed I could point out that part of the problem could be her mad mood swings, but I didn't think this was the best time to bring that into the conversation. "For some people love is hard. And it isn't fair. I totally understand why you were so hurt."

Della leaned against the table behind her. She still had the gun in her hand, but it was pointing at the floor. Now if I could just get her to put it down. It seemed as if she'd forgotten she even held it, so I didn't want to ask her to put it down, which would only remind her of it.

"Sometimes I tell myself I don't need a man," Della said. "I tell myself I'm not only smart and beautiful but I'm independent and strong as well. I tell myself that I'm better off alone, but deep inside I know I'm only lying to myself. I want a man to love me. I need to know I'm the most important person in the world to a man who only has eyes for me." Della looked at me. "Is that so wrong?"

I shook my head. "No. It isn't wrong." I took a step forward. "Love is confusing. It's messy and doesn't always make sense." I took another step forward. Della seemed lost in her thoughts and didn't notice me. "I don't know why love comes easily for some and is evasive for others. In a perfect world, the two halves of every whole would find the other easily and without heartache." I was just one step away from being close enough to grab the gun. "You *are* a smart and beautiful person, and I can see you're strong and independent as well." I took a deep breath and wrapped my hand over Della's hand, which was still hanging on to the gun. I thought I had things under control until I heard the shot.

Chapter 10

Zak pulled me into his arms the minute he arrived. I couldn't help but notice the look of panic on his face when he noticed the blood covering my hands.

"My God, are you okay?" Zak pulled back just a bit and looked me in the eye.

"I'm fine. The blood isn't mine." I looked toward the double doors of the emergency room, where I'd been waiting. "The blood is Della's. It's a long story, but she killed Will, and when I figured out what happened she pulled a gun on me. I managed to distract her and grab the hand that held the gun, but somehow Della was shot in the foot. I brought her here and then called you. You didn't answer, so I left a message."

Zak pulled me against his chest and gave me a hard squeeze. "Your message just said you were at the hospital and would be late coming home. You might have provided a bit more detail. You nearly gave me a heart attack."

"I'm sorry. I guess I figured you'd get the message and call me back."

"I did."

I looked at my phone. There were seven missed calls from Zak. "Oops. I guess my ringer's off."

Zak led me over to a row of sofas. We sat down. "Have you called Salinger?" he asked.

I nodded. "He's on his way."

I felt him relax a bit. I was sorry I'd caused him worry. I should have assured him when I called that I was fine, but we'd just arrived and I was in the middle of getting Della checked in and I guess I just hurried through what I should have known would be an upsetting message for Zak to receive.

"The kids?" I asked.

"I left Alex in charge, but I called Ellie and she and Levi were heading over."

"I guess they should have anticipated the Zoe-gets-herself-into-trouble scenario when they decided to go home before Will's killer was behind bars. I know coming back was inconvenient, but this is really on them for not looking ahead," I said in a light voice that I hoped would turn Zak's frown into a smile.

Zak turned and looked at me, his expression angry. "You promised no sleuthing on your own."

I held up both hands. "I didn't. I swear. I was at the store getting the stuff for the burgers just like I said I would be. When I came out Della was standing by her car with the hood up. She said it wouldn't start. I offered to help her get a tow truck, but she had ice cream in her bag and wanted to get home. What could I do but give her a ride? When we got to her place I helped her carry in her bags. It was then I saw the photo of her and Will in Florida."

"So you confronted her."

I shook my head vigorously. "I didn't. I started to walk to the door the minute the lightbulb went on and I realized what had probably happened. But you know how I really, really don't have a poker face. She realized I'd figured out what I had and pulled the gun on me."

Zak looked at me as if he was trying to decide if I was really as innocent as I claimed. Not that I blamed him. I'd knowingly barreled into danger a number of times in the past, so I imagined there was no reason for him to believe I hadn't somehow brought this on myself. I was on the verge of begging for forgiveness when Salinger walked in. I explained everything that had happened once again and he left to speak to the doctor. A short while later, Salinger came out to tell us they were going to hold Della overnight and we should go.

"It really is kind of sad," I said as Zak drove us home.

"The fact that Will is dead is more than kind of sad," Zak replied.

"I know, and I didn't mean that. I meant it was kind of sad that Della craved permanence and a relationship like we have but could never seem to find it, no matter how hard she tried."

Zak took my hand in his. He rested our joined hands on the seat between us. "Yes," he agreed. "It is sad. Unrequited love totally sucks."

I laughed. "Like you'd know anything about unrequited love. You're handsome and rich and could most likely have any woman you ever wanted. Even in high school, before you were rich, you were confident, smart, and popular. Girls followed you everywhere. You could have had your pick of the litter."

"I didn't want any of those girls. I only wanted you and you hated me," Zak reminded me. His voice sounded a lot more serious than I liked.

I turned so I was facing him. "I didn't hate you. You were just so perfect and so arrogant, which I'll admit I found quite irritating."

Zak smiled and squeezed my hand. "You called me a nerd for more than three years. Never Zak. Always 'hey nerd boy.'"

I shrugged. "Just a cute pet name."

"I hardly thought so. Not at the time at least. I seem to remember you telling me you loathed me and wished I would move away more than once."

"I'm sorry. I guess that was kind of mean."

"That's okay. I wasn't worried. I knew I'd eventually wear you down with my dogged determination, rugged good looks, and superior intellect."

I laughed. "As if."

It was true Zak had been in to me long before I had been in to him, but it wasn't his good looks, intellect, or money that changed my mind. It was his kind and generous heart that caught my attention and made me take another look at the man I'd once thought to be my archnemesis. I had a lot of amazing and loving people in my life, but more than anyone I'd ever met, Zak let his heart rule his actions. He paid close attention when he interacted with others and had a unique way of knowing what people needed, whether they told him or not. Once he knew what someone was lacking he made a point of being there to give it to them. I really, truly loved this man.

"I'm starving," Zak said as we pulled onto our private road.

"I left the burger stuff in my car, which is still at the hospital."

"We'll call for pizza and get your car tomorrow. Before we do anything, though, I think you should wash up. You may not have been injured, but you look like an accident victim."

I glanced down at the blood all over the front of my shirt. "Yeah. That might be a good idea. You know," I said as I leaned over and kissed Zak on the cheek, "I'm in the market for a nerd to wash my back. I don't suppose you know anyone who might be willing to help out a woman who's had a very hard day?"

Zak grinned. "I think I might know a nerd who'd be willing to help you out with that. For a price, of course."

"Oh," I said. "And what price did this nerd have in mind?"

Zak whispered in my ear.

I grinned. "I think you have yourself a deal, nerd boy."

Chapter 11

Easter Sunday

"It looks like Morgan Rose is having a blast," I said to Jeremy as we watched his daughter hunt for Easter eggs with the rest of the kids.

"She is, I think mostly because she's happy her BFF Harper is back. She really missed her when she was away."

I smiled as Eli crawled over and picked up a plastic egg, then immediately began to chew on it. "The girls have been best friends almost since birth, having been born just a few days apart. I'm sure a month was a long time to be without your best bud when you're her age."

"It was hard that she didn't understand how far away Switzerland is." Jeremy ran a hand through his long dark hair to brush it from his eyes. "She kept trying to convince me to take her over to Harper's grandparents' so she could see her, but as hard as I tried to explain the distance thing, she wasn't having any of it."

"It was the first time since she's been old enough to really understand that her friend is gone that Harper has been away for so long. Maybe you can take Morgan on a trip so she can get a feel for how far it is from the other side."

"Actually, now that you mention it, Jessica and I have discussed taking the girls to Disneyland before the new baby is born. I wasn't sure I could take a whole week off, but Aspen is doing great and Tiffany isn't going to part time until June, so we thought maybe we'd try for next month, if that works for you, of course."

Aspen Wood was the latest full-time employee at Zoe's Zoo and Tiffany Middleton was Jeremy's second in command, or at least she would be until she got married.

"I think that's a wonderful idea. And doing it before the baby comes is smart. Zak volunteered to work from home a couple of days a week to be with Catherine if I wanted to return to work part time. I've been thinking maybe it's time. I miss being around the animals on a regular basis."

"That's great." Jeremy grinned. "I think Morgan and Rosalie are both going to love Disneyland. I'll talk to Tiffany and Aspen and we'll figure out the best week for us to go."

"Daddy, can you come help me?" Morgan asked, running up with a basket full of eggs and candy.

"It looks like I'm being paged," Jeremy said. "I'll chat with you later."

I looked around the room for Zak, who, the last time I checked, was carrying Catherine in the front pack while he supervised the older kids, some of whom had wandered onto the beach. Levi was tailing Eli, but I hadn't seen Ellie in almost half an hour. Deciding to check the kitchen, I headed in that direction.

"I thought I might find you in here," I said to her as she stirred mayonnaise into the potato salad. "The food can wait. You should be outside enjoying Eli's first egg hunt."

"I was outside for a while, but then I remembered I still needed to finish a few things before we served dinner. It seems like everyone is having a good time."

I narrowed my gaze. "What's up?"

Ellie smiled. "Why would you think anything's up?"

"I know you. As wonderful a hostess as you are, I don't for a moment believe you'd miss Eli's first egg hunt to make potato salad."

Ellie sighed and stopped stirring. "I never could put anything over on you."

"So what is it?" I asked again.

Ellie glanced down. She'd started to tear up but was unsuccessfully trying to fight back whatever emotion she was feeling.

I walked around the counter and took the spoon out of Ellie's hand. I set it down and took her by the shoulders, then turned her so she was facing me. "What is it?" I asked with real concern in my voice.

Ellie didn't answer right away.

"Come on, El. Tell me. You're really scaring me."

Ellie glanced up and looked me in the eye. "I'm pregnant."

My first reaction was shock, followed quickly by disbelief. "Are you sure?"

Ellie nodded, squeezing her lips together in an effort, I imagined, not to cry. "I think so. I took a test this morning. It was positive."

"Okay," I said, struggling for the right thing to say. "So this is good news?" I had no idea what Ellie thought about having another baby, but based on the tears, I was thinking this wasn't welcome news.

"It's not bad news, but I'm not sure it's good news either." Ellie used a hand to wipe a tear from her cheek. "Eli won't celebrate his first birthday for another three weeks and Levi mentioned just this morning how much he was looking forward to him becoming more independent and moving out of the baby stage."

"You don't think Levi wants more kids?"

Ellie shook her head. "No. I think he does. At least one more. But we both thought having another baby was something we'd do when Eli was a little older. Having two kids in diapers at the same time isn't going to be easy."

No, I supposed it wasn't. Still, I smiled. "Ellie," I said cupping her face with my hands, "you're going to have a baby." I hugged my best friend. "I know he or she may be making an earlier appearance than you planned, but in the long run having a sibling close to your own age is going to be wonderful for both your children."

"You think so?" Ellie asked.

"I know so."

Ellie hugged me hard and long. "Thank you. I don't know how you do it, but you always make me feel better."

"Part of the best friend job description."

Ellie squeezed my hand. "And I appreciate it. But do me a favor: don't tell Levi."

"Oh no." I took a step back. "I'm not promising that again."

Ellie laughed. "I don't mean don't *ever* tell him like I did last time. I just meant don't tell him today. I think he's going to freak out a bit and I don't want this to ruin his day. I'll tell him tomorrow. I promise."

"Okay. I guess I can agree to that." I handed Ellie a tissue. "If you don't want him to suspect something's wrong, though, you should dry your eyes and head out and enjoy the party. The food can wait."

Ellie dabbed her eyes with the tissue. "You're right. The food can wait." Ellie hugged me again. "I don't know what I'd do without you."

I watched as Ellie headed back out to the party with a lightness in her step. I was about to join her when Zak joined me.

"Is everything okay?" he asked.

"Everything's fine. Ellie just needed to talk to me about something. I was about to head out."

Zak pulled me into his arms. "As long as I have you alone…" He pulled me toward him and kissed me on the lips. Catherine, who was still in the front pack on Zak's chest, squealed with delight at the fun game of smush-the-baby Mommy and Daddy were playing with her. Zak took a step back and we both laughed.

"Have you thought about another kid?" I asked Zak.

He looked surprised by my question. "Now?"

"No, silly." I playfully hit him on the arm. "One infant at a time is plenty. I meant, have you thought about having a second baby at some point? We do already have three children we're responsible for. Do you think four would be too many?"

Zak took my hand in his. "I'd like to have more babies with you. I know we never settled on a number, but I've always thought a half dozen or so would be fun."

"Six babies?" I screeched. "You aren't serious!"

Zak grinned. "If we had six babies I'd love and cherish every one of them. But no, I wasn't actually thinking of having quite that many children. But one or two more after Catherine gets a little older would seem just about perfect."

"Okay." I took a step toward the door.

"That's it? You bring up a subject as important as the number of children we'll have and then end the conversation with *okay*?"

I turned back to Zak and put my arms around his neck, once again cradling Catherine between us. "I would love for us to add another baby or two to our family when the time is right."

Zak kissed me on the nose. "Okay," he said and took a step back. He took my hand in his and the three Donovan-Zimmermans headed out to join the party.

Coming next from Kathi Daley Books

Chapter 1

Monday, May 21

I could hear the whispering long before I arrived. It started as a nagging in the back of my mind that grew to a symphony of voices calling me home. I'd felt the echo of what I'd left behind as I made the long trip from one coast to the other.

It had been ten years since I'd stood on this ground. Ten years since I'd heard the voices, felt the connection, seen the images of those who had come before. When I left Cutter's Cove a decade ago, I knew I would return. What I didn't know was how long my return would take.

I stood on the bluff overlooking the angry sea. The sky was dark, with heavy clouds that blocked what was left of the afternoon sun. The rumbling in the distance informed me that a storm was rolling toward shore, but it was the murmurs from the house that caused a chill to run down my spine.

I pulled my sweater tightly around my thin frame as the wind raged from the west. My blond hair blew across my face as I tried to emotionally confront the nightmare that had demanded my return. A good friend had died, brutally murdered in his own home. After six months his killer still roamed free. This, I'd decided, was something I couldn't bear.

"I'm here," I whispered as the air became heavy with the approaching storm. Lightning flashed across the sky and still I waited. The house had once been my sanctuary, but now, after all this time, I was hesitant to find out who waited impatiently for my return.

I closed my eyes and listened as the waves crashed onto the rocky shore beneath me. I could feel a presence and wondered if my ability to see those who had passed on had been restored now that I'd returned to the house. It wasn't as if I was born with the ability to see ghosts. I hadn't, in fact, seen my first one until I'd moved from New York to Cutter's Cove, Oregon, at the age of sixteen. At the time I believed the gift was the result of some sort of personal growth, but when I moved away from the house and away from the sea, the images faded.

My phone rang, and I turned back toward my Mercedes. I'd promised my mother I'd call when I arrived, so I hurried to the car. I opened the passenger side door and grabbed the phone, which had been resting on the charger.

"Are you there?" Mom asked from the other end of the phone line.

"I'm here."

"How's the house? Ten years is a long time to go without any type of maintenance."

I looked toward the large home that Mom and I had bought and fixed up twelve years ago. We'd found the house—or perhaps the house had found us—during one of the most difficult times in our lives. Spending time together renovating the dilapidated old lady had not only been cathartic but life changing as well. "I haven't been inside, but from the outside she looks just as I remember. She needs a coat of paint, but it seems she's stood strong while she waited."

"Are you sure about this?" Mom asked for the hundredth time.

"I'm sure." I looked out toward the sea. "It's been six months since Booker's death. I spoke to Woody Baker," I said, "and the police are no closer to solving the case than they were on the day his body was found."

"I understand. I really do. But your life is in New York now. Doesn't it feel strange to return to the place where everyone knew you as Alyson?"

I paused before I answered. An image of Alyson flashed through my mind. Although we'd shared the same body, in many ways she felt like a totally different person. When I'd lived in Cutter's Cove a decade ago, I'd used the name Alyson Prescott, a persona I'd been assigned when my mom and I had been placed in the witness protection program. My real name is Amanda Parker, a name I resumed when the men who wanted me dead were murdered themselves. "Yes," I admitted. "It does feel strange. But I have to do this."

"You know I'll support you, whatever you decide."

I smiled. "I know. And I love you for it." I felt a heavy weight settle in my chest. Deciding that serious conversations could wait for another day, I changed the subject. "How's Tucker doing? Didn't he have his checkup today?" Tucker was my German shepherd who stayed with Mom when I went away to college nine years ago. After college I'd secured a high-paying job in a very competitive industry and was rarely home, so Tucker had continued to live with my mother. He was twelve years old now and showing signs of slowing down.

"The vet said he's doing really well for a dog his age. She gave me supplements as well as some mild pain meds to help with the arthritis."

I let out a sigh of relief. "Good. I was worried about him. Give him a kiss for me and tell him I love him."

"Always."

I glanced back toward the house. "I should get inside and try to get the electricity and heat on before the storm arrives. I'm not sure if I'll have reception once it does, so don't worry if you can't get hold of me."

"Okay. Be careful."

I smiled as the reality of my mother's unconditional love warmed my heart. "I will. I love you. I'll call you tomorrow."

I opened the glove box and grabbed the keys to the house. When Mom and I had first come to Cutter's Cove and found the house perched on the edge of the sea, we'd known we were home. Sure, it had stood empty since the death of the previous owner, and admittedly, it had been about as dilapidated as a house could be and still be standing, but it had history and character and as far as we were concerned, it was love at first sight. Hoping the key would work in the old lock, I slipped it into the door. Luckily, it turned without effort and I stepped inside.

Finally, I heard the house whisper.

I'm not sure how to explain what I felt in that moment. A sense of homecoming, for sure, but also a hollowness I couldn't quite explain. The furniture Mom and I had taken such care to choose was covered with sheets and every other surface was covered with dust. I took a step forward, batting at the tapestry of cobwebs that hung from the ceiling.

I took several more steps into the interior. "Is anyone there?" I said out loud. I hadn't seen anyone, but the sense that I wasn't alone was overwhelming.

As I stood silently and listened, memories I thought long buried suddenly consumed me. When Mom and I had first come to Cutter's Cove I'd been so lost. My best friend had just been murdered and Mom and I had been forced to flee the life we'd always known because the men who'd committed the murder had identified me, the only witness to a gangland shooting. I'd thought leaving Amanda Parker behind would be both painful and confusing, and it was, but I found Alyson's easygoing approach to life surprisingly refreshing. During the two years I'd lived as Alyson, I rarely thought of Amanda, yet it hadn't been all that difficult to reclaim my old life when I returned to the place where Amanda's had been the only identity I'd ever known.

"Is anyone there?" I repeated as I saw a movement out of the corner of my eye.

I paused, but no one answered. I supposed it could just be a trick of the light.

The gas and electrical turnoffs were in the basement, so I headed in that direction. The house was huge and so very different from anything we'd known in New York, with nine fireplaces spread among three floors of living space. There was also a basement and a finished attic. Mom, an artist, had replaced the wall on the ocean side of the attic with windows and had turned the space into a studio. She never spoke of it now that she'd resumed her old life, but I often pictured her there, standing at the window, looking out to sea with a contemplative look on her face.

As I entered the main living area I glanced at the painting on the wall. Mom had captured me and my two best friends, Mackenzie Reynolds and Trevor Johnson, in an unsuspecting moment and converted the photo to oil. When I'd left Cutter's Cove ten years ago I'd promised Mac and Trevor that I'd come back to visit all the time. I promised we'd text and Skype every day, and one day find our way back to one another. And we had texted and Skyped. At first. But as the weeks turned into months, and the months into years, we'd become busy with our own lives and drifted apart.

A rustling overhead caused me to pause and listen. It could be animals who'd found their way into the house, though the last time I'd heard strange noises overhead it hadn't been animals at all.

"Hello," I called, louder this time. "Is someone there?"

There was no answer and the rustling stopped, so I continued into the kitchen. I focused on the clickety-clack of my heels hitting the deep blue tile floor as I crossed the room. At the stairs leading down to the basement, I turned on the flashlight on my phone and made my way into the inky darkness of the damp room. When we'd first moved into the house, the space beneath the first floor had been cluttered with remnants from previous residents, as had the attic. Mom and I had cleared out both spaces and now the basement was mostly empty. My first stop was the electrical box. I'd called the power company a few days before to have the power turned on and hoped all that would be required to bathe the house in light would be a flip of the switch.

"Voilà!" I said as the power came on.

Now all I had to do was turn on the gas and I might be looking at a hot shower that evening. I'd been driving for days, but the journey seemed little more than a blur in my consciousness. Once I'd started the drive west I'd felt the pull of the voices and had thought about little else. After confirming that the gas was working I went back upstairs to the first floor. It would take me a couple of days of elbow grease before the place was habitable, but for now I had plumbing and a place to stay. I'd brought an ice chest with a few necessities as well as coffee and wine, so it seemed I could survive the night.

I was about to head upstairs to check out my room when my phone rang. I pulled it out of my pocket and looked at the caller ID. My first reaction was annoyance that my life in New York had found a way to intrude on my first minutes back in Cutter's Cove, then realized how irrational that was and answered. "Ethan. I was just going to call you," I said to my boyfriend of two years, Ethan Wentworth.

"Have you arrived?"

"I have."

"And how did you find it?"

"I mostly remembered how to get here."

Ethan didn't speak for a moment. I knew he was confused by my response, but I couldn't help but tease him after the way he had framed his question. Ethan was a wonderful person and a kind and considerate boyfriend, but he was a product of old money and a rigid upbringing that resulted in a precise way of moving and speaking.

"I'm just kidding." I laughed. "I found the house to be dusty but intact. How did your court case go?"

"Fine. Our case was impenetrable."

"So you won?"

"Yes. I believe I just said that."

I smiled. "You did, and I'm proud of you. I knew you would tear the place up with your research."

Ethan was a junior partner for one of the top law firms in New York, while I worked as a graphic designer for one of the top advertising agencies.

"Have you had a chance to talk to your policeman friend?" Ethan asked.

"No. I'll track Woody down tomorrow. Right now, I'm exhausted. I just want to settle in, take a hot shower, and maybe have a glass of wine."

"I ran into Skip and Gina today," Ethan said without a beat. He obviously hadn't picked up on her subtle hint that maybe they should sign off now. "They're planning a party next month to celebrate Skip's promotion and their purchase of the new yacht. They asked if you'd be back by then. I told them I thought you would."

I couldn't help but notice his tone made it a question rather than a statement. "I took a six-week leave from the office, but if I get things wrapped up sooner I'll certainly come home sooner. Still, I don't think I can commit to a party in just a few weeks. I'll have to let you know."

"Are you sure about this venture you've embarked on? You realize it's not your responsibility to find this man's killer."

"Of course it isn't. Still, I think I can help."

"How? I understand he was your friend and his murder has gone unsolved and that makes you sad and angry. But really, Amanda, how can you help?"

I hesitated. Ethan didn't know about my ability to see ghosts. He'd never understand, and I knew I could never tell him. That part of me belonged to Alyson. Ethan was part of Amanda's world. "It's hard to explain. Listen, I have to go. I'll call you tomorrow."

Ethan let out a breath that sounded a lot like frustration. "All right. Be careful."

"I will." I hung up and held the phone to my chest. Ethan didn't understand, and I supposed I didn't blame him. I slipped the phone into my pocket and went toward the stairs. I'd just begun my ascent when a flash of something caught my eye. "Hello," I called once again. "Is someone there?"

There was still no answer, but I was pretty sure what I was seeing and hearing wasn't an animal. "Barkley?" I asked. Barkley Cutter had been the previous owner of the house and the first ghost I had seen after moving to Cutter's Cove. "Is that you? Are you here?"

There was no answer, but Barkley had never answered in the past. My ability to communicate with ghosts had been limited to seeing them. I'd never been able to speak to them. I was pretty sure Barkley had moved on once my friends and I had solved his murder and found his grandson, so the flash I kept seeing most likely wasn't him.

I supposed any number of spirits could have moved into the house during the decade I'd been gone. In my experience if they wanted to make contact they would, so I continued to walk on. When I reached the landing to the second floor I glanced toward the room that had been my mother's. It felt odd to be in the house without her, but she was busy with her new life, or maybe I should say the resumption of her old one. I took a moment to remember the way things had been when we'd first purchased the house, then went to my own room. When I opened the door I expected to see sheets and cobwebs, as elsewhere, but what I found instead was someone lounging on my bed.

"Who are you?" I asked the apparition, who looked exactly like me. A younger version of me, but me nonetheless.

"I'm Alyson. Who are you?"

"Amanda. What are you?" The form really did look like me, although she was translucent, like a ghost. Somehow, I didn't think she *was* a ghost. For one thing, I wasn't dead. For another, I could speak to her *and* hear her response.

Alyson laid back against the pillow and lifted her legs into the air. She stared at her feet, which were in line with her hips, as if they were the most interesting thing she'd ever seen. "I'm not totally clear on this, but I think I'm the part of you that you left behind."

I narrowed my gaze. "You're part of me? Have you been here this whole time?"

Alyson shrugged. "I guess. What has it been, a couple of weeks?"

"Ten years."

"Damn, girl. I had no idea." Alyson sat up and crossed her legs. "No wonder I'm so bored. Things have been kinda dead around here since you left."

I frowned.

"Get it? Dead around here?" Alyson giggled.

I tossed the Michael Kors bag that held my overnight things on the floor and then sat on the edge of the bed. A white sheet still covered the mattress. "You look like me, but you don't sound like me. I left here when I was seventeen, and even though I was a teenager, I certainly didn't talk or act the way you do."

"What can I say? What you see is the new and improved version of Alyson."

I frowned. "How is that possible? Even if by some weird chance the part of me that's somehow connected to this house remained behind when I left, why on earth would it have a completely different personality?"

Alyson shrugged. "I guess Amanda took all the stodgy, boring, elitist stuff with her and what was left behind were all the best parts. Did you bring food?"

"Do you eat?"

Alyson's smile faded. "Unfortunately, no. But I can remember what it was like when I was you and you were me and we were one. It's been a while."

"If I eat will you be able to enjoy it?"

"I have no idea, but I'd love to try." Alyson tilted her head. Her long blond hair swept the mattress. I missed my long hair. At some point along the way I'd decided a woman of my age needed to present a more professional appearance, so I'd cut it. Not super short. Around shoulder length.

I closed my eyes and took several deep breaths. I still wasn't sure if Alyson was real. For all I knew, I was suffering the effects of driving three thousand miles in four days.

"I know what you're thinking," Alyson said. "And I can assure you, I'm real."

I opened my eyes. "How did you know what I was thinking?"

"Duh." Alyson rolled her eyes. "I'm you, remember? And no…" Alyson got up and began jumping up and down on the bed. "You aren't going crazy. And yes, you'll eventually come to love me."

Now I was sure I was having a hallucination. I never jumped on beds as Amanda *or* Alyson. Not even when I was a young child. Jumping on beds was something people like me simply didn't do. "I'm going out to the car to get the rest of my things. I assume you'll be gone when I get back."

Alyson got down off the bed. "Amanda, Amanda, Amanda. How do I make you understand? I'm not going anywhere. I live here. Haven't you been paying attention?"

"I've been paying attention, but that doesn't mean I have to accept what I'm seeing. If you were me, you would act like me. Because you don't, my only conclusion is that you're a figment of my imagination."

Alyson walked over to me. We were exactly the same height, so her blue eyes looked directly into mine. "What happened to you? Don't you remember being Alyson? Don't you remember wearing jeans and going barefoot and having fun? Don't you remember how happy you were once you were able to shed Amanda and her zillions of dollars, private schools, and designer shoes that felt like torture every minute you wore them?"

I glanced down at the pantsuit I was wearing with matching pumps. I really was dying to kick them off and pull on some baggy sweats. Of course, Amanda didn't own baggy sweats. "I do remember," I said. "But that wasn't real. Alyson wasn't real. It was as if I took a vacation from my life, but somewhere inside I knew Amanda was always there waiting to come out when it was safe to do so."

Alyson shrugged. "Suit yourself. If you're going to empty that fancy car of yours that probably cost more than you paid for this house, you'd better hurry. It's starting to rain."

Ghost me was right. It was starting to rain. I paused for just a moment and then hurried down the stairs to get the things I'd left in my trunk. When I returned she was gone. Perhaps she'd been an illusion after all.

Recipes

Baked Fruit Pie—submitted by Nancy Farris
Peanut Butter Chess Pie—submitted by Jean Daniel
No Name Cake—submitted by Patty Liu
Lemon Tea Cookies—submitted by Vivian Shane

Baked Fruit Pie

Submitted by Nancy Farris

This is a go-to when I need to take a side dish to a party. There won't be another one like it there and there won't be a drop of it left!

1 stick (½ cup) unsalted butter, melted, plus 1 tbs. to coat casserole
½ cup packed light brown sugar
6 tbs. flour
8 oz. shredded sharp cheddar cheese
1 20-oz. can pineapple chunks in pineapple juice, drained into a measuring cup. Reserve 6 tbs. juice.
1 20-oz. can sliced peaches, drained and cut in chunks about the size of the pineapple chunks
1 cup crushed Ritz crackers

Preheat oven to 350°. Butter a 2-qt. casserole dish and set aside.

In a large bowl, mix together the brown sugar and flour. Stir in the cheese. Add the pineapple and peach chunks and stir until combined. Pour into casserole dish.

In a small bowl, mix together the melted butter, reserved pineapple juice, and the cracker crumbs. Stir until well blended.

Sprinkle the crumb mixture over the fruit mixture.

Bake at 350° for 30–40 min. or until brown and bubbling. Let stand 5 min. before serving.

Peanut Butter Chess Pie

Submitted by Jean Daniel

This is a great pie for Easter or Sunday dinner, which is what my family uses it for.

1 unbaked pie crust
½ cup butter (1 stick), melted
½ cup creamy peanut butter
4 eggs
1½ cups sugar
2 tbs. cornmeal
1 tbs. flour
1 tbs. white vinegar
1 tbs. vanilla

Heat oven to 350°.
Stir the melted butter and the peanut butter together until smooth. Whisk in the eggs, sugar, cornmeal, flour, vinegar, and vanilla. Pour all into crust and bake for 50 min. or until browned. It will still jiggle in the middle a little. Really good with a scoop of vanilla ice cream.

No Name Cake

Submitted by Patty Liu

1 pkg. yellow cake mix
1 large can pineapple, crushed
1 cup sugar
1 pkg. (6-serving size) Jell-O *Instant* Vanilla Pudding mix; prepare according to package directions
1 large container Cool Whip, thawed
Flaked coconut (toasted, if desired)

Prepare according to directions and bake cake in a 2 x 9 x 13-inch pan. Bring pineapple and sugar to a boil, then let cool completely. Once baked cake has cooled, poke holes in it with a fork and pour pineapple mixture over it; drain excess juice prior to pouring over cake. Spread prepared pudding over top of pineapple layer; refrigerate. Shortly before serving, spread Cool Whip over cake and sprinkle with coconut, if desired.

Serves 12 to 14

Lemon Tea Cookies

Submitted by Vivian Shane

These cookies taste like little lemon cakes. I made them for Mother's Day brunch for many years and more recently for a "grown-up" tea party with my girlfriends.

½ cup milk
2¼ tsp. lemon juice
1¾ cups flour
1 tsp. baking powder
¼ tsp. baking soda
¼ tsp. salt
½ cup butter
1½ cup sugar
1 egg
1 tsp. finely shredded lemon peel

Stir together milk and 2 tsp. lemon juice and set aside. Stir together the flour, baking powder, baking soda, and salt. In a large bowl, beat the butter until softened. Add ¾ cup sugar and beat until fluffy. Add egg and lemon peel and beat well. Add flour mixture and milk mixture, alternately beating until well mixed. Drop by rounded teaspoon onto an ungreased cookie sheet. Bake at 350° oven for 12–14 min. Meanwhile, stir together ¾ cup sugar and ¼ cup lemon juice until well combined. Remove cookies from oven and immediately brush with lemon mixture. Cool and enjoy!

Books by Kathi Daley

Come for the murder, stay for the romance.

Zoe Donovan Cozy Mystery:

Halloween Hijinks
The Trouble With Turkeys
Christmas Crazy
Cupid's Curse
Big Bunny Bump-off
Beach Blanket Barbie
Maui Madness
Derby Divas
Haunted Hamlet
Turkeys, Tuxes, and Tabbies
Christmas Cozy
Alaskan Alliance
Matrimony Meltdown
Soul Surrender
Heavenly Honeymoon
Hopscotch Homicide
Ghostly Graveyard
Santa Sleuth
Shamrock Shenanigans
Kitten Kaboodle
Costume Catastrophe
Candy Cane Caper
Holiday Hangover
Easter Escapade
Camp Carter

Trick or Treason
Reindeer Roundup
Hippity Hoppity Homicide

Zimmerman Academy The New Normal
Ashton Falls Cozy Cookbook

Tj Jensen Paradise Lake Mysteries by Henery Press:
Pumpkins in Paradise
Snowmen in Paradise
Bikinis in Paradise
Christmas in Paradise
Puppies in Paradise
Halloween in Paradise
Treasure in Paradise
Fireworks in Paradise
Beaches in Paradise – *July 2018*

Whales and Tails Cozy Mystery:
Romeow and Juliet
The Mad Catter
Grimm's Furry Tail
Much Ado About Felines
Legend of Tabby Hollow
Cat of Christmas Past
A Tale of Two Tabbies
The Great Catsby
Count Catula
The Cat of Christmas Present
A Winter's Tail
The Taming of the Tabby
Frankencat

The Cat of Christmas Future
Farewell to Felines

Writers' Retreat Southern Seashore Mystery:
First Case
Second Look
Third Strike
Fourth Victim
Fifth Night
Sixth Cabin – *May 2018*

Rescue Alaska Paranormal Mystery:
Finding Justice
Finding Answers – *May 2018*

A Tess and Tilly Mystery:
The Christmas Letter
The Valentine Mystery
The Mother's Day Mishap – *April 2018*

Sand and Sea Hawaiian Mystery:
Murder at Dolphin Bay
Murder at Sunrise Beach
Murder at the Witching Hour
Murder at Christmas
Murder at Turtle Cove
Murder at Water's Edge
Murder at Midnight

Seacliff High Mystery:

The Secret
The Curse
The Relic
The Conspiracy
The Grudge
The Shadow
The Haunting

Haunting by the Sea:

Homecoming by the Sea – *April 2018*

Road to Christmas Romance:

Road to Christmas Past

USA Today best-selling author Kathi Daley lives in beautiful Lake Tahoe with her husband Ken. When she isn't writing, she likes spending time hiking the miles of desolate trails surrounding her home. She has authored more than seventy-five books in eight series, including Zoe Donovan Cozy Mysteries, Whales and Tails Island Mysteries, Sand and Sea Hawaiian Mysteries, Tj Jensen Paradise Lake Series, Writers' Retreat Southern Seashore Mysteries, Rescue Alaska Paranormal Mysteries, and Seacliff High Teen Mysteries. Find out more about her books at **www.kathidaley.com**

Stay up to date:
Newsletter, *The Daley Weekly* **http://eepurl.com/NRPDf**
Kathi Daley Blog - **http://kathidaleyblog.com**
Webpage – **www.kathidaley.com**
Facebook at Kathi Daley Books –
www.facebook.com/kathidaleybooks
Kathi Daley Books Group Page –
https://www.facebook.com/groups/569578823146850/
E-mail – **kathidaley@kathidaley.com**
Twitter – **https://twitter.com/kathidaley**
Amazon –**https://www.amazon.com/author/kathidaley**
BookBub – **https://www.bookbub.com/authors/kathi-daley**

71659616R00104

Made in the USA
San Bernardino, CA
18 March 2018